D1591430

STAY OUT OF THE SHOWER

William Schoell

STAY OUT OF THE SHOWER

25 Years of Shocker Films Beginning with "Psycho"

DEMBNER BOOKS

NEW YORK

Dembner Books
Published by Red Dembner Enterprises Corp., 80 Eighth Avenue, New York, N.Y. 10011
Distributed by W. W. Norton & Company, Inc., 500 Fifth Avenue, New York, N. Y. 10110

Library of Congress Cataloging in Publication Data

Schoell, William.
    Stay out of the shower

    Includes index.
    1. Horror films—History and criticism.   2. Horror films—Psychological aspects.   I. Title.
PN1995.9.H6S34   1985   791.43′09′0916   85-4477
ISBN 0-934878-61-7 (pbk.)

FOR LAWRENCE J. QUIRK

ACKNOWLEDGMENTS

Special thanks to: Lawrence J. Quirk, Doug McClelland, John A. Guzman; Dorothy Swerdlove, Dr. Rod Bladel, and the staff of the Billy Rose Theatre Collection, Museum of Performing Arts, Lincoln Center, New York; Jerry Ohlinger's Movie Material Store, New York.

With appreciation also to: Universal-MCA; Renaissance Pictures, Ltd.; Shamley Productions, Inc.; Paramount Pictures Corp.; Columbia Pictures; Screen Gems, Inc.; Amicus Productions, Ltd.; Metro-Goldwyn-Mayer, Inc.; RKO-International; Avco Embassy; United Artists Corp.; Warner Brothers; Filmways Pictures, Inc.; Commonwealth United Entertainment, Inc.; Towers of London (Films) Limited; Adult Films; American-International; Cannon Productions; Lorimar Productions, Inc.; International Spectra-film Distribution, Inc.; Tri-Star Pictures; Aquarius Films; Allied Artists; Woolner Brothers; Pacemaker Pictures; International Entertainment Corp.; Constitution Films; Atlantic Releasing Corp.; Filmplan International Two; New World Pictures; 20th Century-Fox; SLM Entertainment, Ltd.; Laurel Productions; UM Film Distribution; Sandy Howard Productions; Bryanston Productions; The Associates and Aldrich Co. Productions; Seven Arts-Hammer Productions; Mayflower Pictures, Inc.; Compass International; Dino De Laurentiis Corp.; Orion Pictures; The Ladd Company; Pressman Williams Enterprises, Inc.; 21st Century Distributing Corp.; Magnum Motion Pictures; Maniac Productions; Fiducial Resource International, Inc., Analysis Film Corporation.

And with special thanks to Therese Eiben and S. Arthur Dembner.

All of the motion picture stills in this book come from private collections.

CONTENTS

Norman stands outside the Bates house in *Psycho Two*.

CHAPTER ONE

WHAT IS A SHOCKER?

In 1960[1] a film was introduced to the public that was to forever change the course of film history. Alfred Hitchcock's *Psycho*, damned at the time for its violence in much the same way that current film fare is attacked by some critics, has since gone on to become a classic of the cinema. Made on a low budget, filmed in black and white, and pertaining to gruesome subject matter, it seemed an odd candidate to become one of the most famous motion pictures in the world.

A quarter of a century later people still discuss *Psycho*. It gave birth to literally hundreds of motion pictures that are in some way modeled after it. Dozens of directors have started their own careers by trying to imitate its special qualities. Often, when a new horror movie opens, ads prominently proclaim that it is "comparable to *Psycho*." Imagine. A film over two decades old which is still being imitated, still being used by publicity departments in attempts to excite people the way the original once did, and still does. There was even a *Psycho Two*, made a generation after the original. Now a *Psycho Three* is in the works.

Why has *Psycho* become one of the best-known and best-loved films of all time? Because audiences have long had a love affair with movies they can scream through, movies that manipulate their emotions and purge their fears. Of those movies, *Psycho* is one of the best.

For some deep-down, subconscious reasons that are better left to the psychologists, people love to be shocked. Films that deal with, for example, child pornography, nuclear war, or terminal illness will certainly have shock value, but traditionally the term *shocker* has been used for films that chill the blood rather than for those that generate controversy or general paranoia. Virtually all horror films could be classified as shockers. However, the success of *Psycho* resulted in a new type of multiple-murder film or "psycho-shocker." They are films about madmen—or women—on the loose, stabbing and hacking at allegedly innocent

1

victims. In these films the *depiction* of death is as important as the plot and characters, if not more so. People are elaborately killed under bizarre circumstances, and the filmmakers often spend more time planning out the death scenes than any other.

Multiple-murder films did not begin with *Psycho*, of course. *Psycho* was also not the first film to show someone being murdered. However, all those hundreds of comparatively polite drawing room mysteries, Sherlock Holmes films, creepy "old house" chillers, and forties murder melodramas cannot be classified as shockers. The murders in those films, when they were shown at all, were quite tasteful by today's standards. In mystery films, the unmasking of the killer was the most important part. Haunted house movies chilled their audiences with spooky atmosphere and evocative lighting, not with gruesome murder scenes. Crime melodramas of the forties, such as *The Big Sleep*, had plenty of gunfights and high body counts, but audiences went to them to thrill to the chase and adventure, not to the act of murder.

Throughout the history of the cinema there have been films that shocked their audiences, even films that dealt, like *Psycho*, with the dark, pathological side of human sexuality. None of these earlier movies, however, had the impact *Psycho* had. They did not spawn dozens of imitations, nor did they have any sequences that were as bold and graphic, for its day, as *Psycho*'s shower murder. Even Michael Powell's *Peeping Tom*, which was made at the same time as *Psycho* and was almost as controversial, never became as well known or as widely seen as Hitchcock's film.

Peeping Tom is sometimes classified as a *Psycho* imitation because it was released in this country after *Psycho*. However, it opened in London two months before *Psycho*. Nevertheless, the Hitchcock influence is obvious in the suspense techniques Powell employs. *Variety*'s overseas critic had reservations about *Peeping Tom*'s screenplay and character development, but thought it was a superior chiller. London's critics had a more adverse reaction to *Peeping Tom* than to *Psycho*. The picture was banned for years due to its grim subject matter and sexual overtones, and the distinguished Powell's career was almost destroyed. *Peeping Tom* was unveiled for a whole new audience in 1979 when it was rereleased, uncut, after being shown at the prestigious New York Film Festival.

Peeping Tom is a suspense film about a psychopath who takes movies of his female victims as he kills them, then watches their death throes in the privacy of his room. The film contains a great deal of humor, all of it intentional and most of it black, which serves to diminish its initially distasteful atmosphere. The film's chief flaws are a somewhat draggy pacing, a weak musical score, and some slightly contrived developments toward the end. The movie is not especially scary. Its most frightening moments come when the murderer's past is revealed and the audience learns the circumstances that turned him into the monster, albeit charming and tormented, that he is. Carl Boehm is competent, if a bit wooden, in the role. What lifts the movie above the exploitation level is the interesting script and directorial touches and certain characterizations. Anna Massey is particularly memorable as the young woman downstairs who falls for Boehm without realizing what he's up to. The final sequence reveals what it is that accounts for the victims' extra-horrified death expressions: Boehm has attached a mirror to the device with which he stabs them, so that they can *watch themselves die!* This grotesque touch had a lot to do with the public's appalled reaction to this movie, which should not be left out of any list of notable shockers.

Some of the memorable films of the thirties and forties that dwelled on lurid subject matter include: the original *Night Must Fall* (1937); *Bewitched* (1945), with Phyllis Thaxter as a deranged woman with split personalities; Robert Siodmak's overrated *The Spiral Staircase* (1946), about a killer who preys only on the handicapped; *The Dark Mirror* (1946), with Olivia de Havilland as twins, one of whom is a psychopathic murderer (the film was later remade for TV with Jane Seymour in the dual role); and *Sorry Wrong Number* (1948), Barbara Stanwyck's tour de force as a bedridden woman who overhears on the telephone a plot to commit her own murder. That final scene—"Henry, there's someone on the stairs!"—will still take your breath away.

The fifties also had quite a few horrific and lurid films. The Hammer Studio's horror movies, with Christopher Lee playing Dracula, and Peter Cushing playing everyone else, opened up new doors of gore in the late fifties—though their violence seems tame and comic-bookish today—but aside from such items as *Paranoiac*, most of these films do not fall under the definition of shocker. *The Unguarded Moment* (1956) concerns a high-school student (John Saxon) who tries to molest a teacher (Esther Williams), and is suspected of committing a series of rape-murders. *Terror in the Haunted House* (1958) revolves around (unseen) axe murders—committed in the attic of a wedding house—which had been witness-ed by the bride as a child. *Horrors in the Black Museum* (1959) is an energetic but suspenseless tale of a mad writer and his assistant who terrorize London by committing a series of fiendish murders. (One buxom woman gets her head sliced off by a guillotine placed above her pillow!)

French filmmaker Henri-Georges Clouzot's *Diabolique* (1955) had audiences literally standing up in their seats and screaming at *its* classic bathroom scene. The body of a man, presumed dead, has been placed in a bathtub. In the climax, the "dead man" rises up in the water and gives his wife a fatal heart attack. *Diabolique*, however, did not have the long-term impact of *Psycho*. The bathtub sequence is not as shocking as what happens to Janet Leigh in the shower.

Two films directed by Gerd Oswald are worthy of comment. *A Kiss Before Dying*

(1956), based on Ira Levin's excellent suspense novel, is a terrific melodrama about a homicidal young man (Robert Wagner) who plans to marry his way into a wealthy family, and is not above murdering people to do so. The murders are juiced for every drop of suspense, with plenty of time given to fully absorb the tragedy of the deaths. The rooftop sequence when Wagner pushes Joanne Woodward to her death is incredibly tense and disturbingly poignant. Gerd Oswald's direction, while not quite up to Hitchcock's, is mostly excellent. There are even some coincidental structural similarities to *Psycho*, which was made four years later.

The other Oswald film, *Screaming Mimi*, made in 1958, was certainly ahead of its time. This involved, farfetched "psychodrama" is based on a Frederic Brown novel. It deals with a beautiful young dancer (Anita Ekberg)—a former mental patient—who runs off with her doctor and gets involved with a newspaperman investigating a slasher murder. It turns out that Ekberg is the killer, and that she gets excited by a fetish statue that her brother had modeled after her. Oswald, however, was apparently not too excited by his material this time, as his direction

Today's shockers are much more graphic.

lacks finesse. The low spot of the picture is when Gypsy Rose Lee croaks out "Put the Blame on Mame".

But who remembers *Screaming Mimi* today? Even the excellent *A Kiss Before Dying* never captured the public imagination and critical attention that *Psycho* did. These earlier films, however important some of them may have been at the time of their release, have not had the impact of *Psycho*, nor have any of them been as influential.

The new approaches to violence, pathology, and sexuality that *Psycho* brought into being have ultimately led to the more graphic shockers of today. Although contemporary "splatter movies"—films in which the emphasis is on graphic, bone-cracking, blood-spurting violence—can include certain westerns, gangster movies, or Kung Fu pictures, the vast majority of them concern mad, slashing psychopaths on the loose. Such films fall under the shocker umbrella, which opened when the profits of *Psycho* (both monetary and cinematic groundbreakers) began to rain in on the film industry.

In the opening of that fateful film in 1960, the seeds for a new generation in the history of film were planted. A quarter of a century later, the shocker film industry has grown to monstrous proportions.

No one will ever say that most of these movies are profound experiences, that they're on a level with such great classics of the cinema as *The Heiress, From Here to Eternity, La Dolce Vita,* or *The Last Picture Show,* but shockers can and often do say things about the human condition, sometimes unappealing things. Many of these films make up for what they lack in profundity by technical proficiency and craftsmanship and the skill with which they delight, chill, and manipulate the audience. That's part of what movies are all about, after all, using the camera on its purest level to evoke feelings strong and terrible.

The best shockers are cinematic experiences that intelligently employ editing, cinematography, and lighting to create a particular effect. Without the strong characters and story lines of plays and novels, shockers rely on the cinema's full bag of tricks to achieve their goal of inducing terror in an audience. These films deserve serious study, if for no other reason than that they have delighted, frightened, and titillated audiences for years, and in all likelihood will continue to do so for many years to come.

THE BIG NEWS IS THAT "PSYCHO" IS HITCHCOCK'S GREATEST CHILLER!

CHAPTER TWO

PSYCHO: THE BEGINNING

Psycho (1960). Produced and directed by Alfred Hitchcock. Screenplay: Joseph Stefano, based on the novel by Robert Bloch. Photography: John L. Russell. Editor: George Tomasini. Art Directors: Joseph Hurley, Robert Clatworthy. Set Decorator: George Milo. Unit Manager: Lew Leary. Titles designed by: Saul Bass. Pictorial Consultant: Saul Bass. Assistant Director: Hilton A. Green. Costume Supervisor: Helen Colvig. Makeup Supervision: Jack Barron and Robert Dawn. Hairstylist: Florence Bush. Special Effects: Clarence Champagne. Sound Recording by Waldon O. Watson and William Russell. Music by Bernard Herrmann. A Paramount release. Running time: 108 minutes. *With*: Janet Leigh (Marion Crane); Anthony Perkins (Norman Bates); Vera Miles (Lila Crane); John Gavin (Sam Loomis); Martin Balsam (Milton Arbogast); John McIntire (Sheriff); Simon Oakland (Dr. Richmond); Frank Albertson (the millionaire); Lurene Tuttle (Sheriff's wife). Also with Patricia Hitchcock, Vaughn Taylor, John Anderson, Mort Mills.

In 1959 Simon and Schuster published a short novel by suspense specialist Robert Bloch entitled *Psycho*. It begins as the story of Mary Crane, a secretary who absconds with $40,000 and checks in at a rundown motel. At the end of the third chapter (of seventeen), Mary steps into a shower stall, turns on the water, and is then beheaded—rather implausibly with one stroke—by a maniac wielding a butcher knife. Reportedly, the novel was partly inspired by the pathological exploits of Ed Gein, a mass murderer who lived in a veritable house of horrors full of preserved human heads and souvenirs of other atrocities. (Gein is even referred to at one point in the novel.) The pictures *Deranged* (1974) and *Texas Chainsaw Massacre* (1974) were also based on Gein's bloody career. Gein

An advertising poster for *Psycho*.

died of cancer at seventy-seven in the Mendota State Hospital in Madison, Wisconsin.

John Russell Taylor reports, in his book *Hitch*: *The Life and Work of Alfred Hitchcock*, that at the time of the novel's publication, Hitchcock had noticed that the biggest cinema moneymakers were sleazy, ineptly made, low-budget horror films.[2] Hitchcock wondered if he could beat these horror moviemakers at their own game. *Psycho*, with the sudden, startling murder of its nominal heroine, seemed like the perfect property to use for his experiment.

Joseph Stefano's screenplay, which was written in close consultation with Hitchcock, made a few departures from the novel. Mary Crane became Marion Crane, and Norman Bates, originally fat, middle-aged, and bespectacled, was turned into a young, slender, and nice-looking fellow, played by Anthony Perkins in the movie. In the novel Norman is introduced on the first page, but his initial appearance in the film occurs half an hour into it. Marion is not beheaded in the shower, as in the book, but repeatedly stabbed in the torso instead. Also, the murder occurs not in a square shower stall but in a bathtub with a showerhead and curtain. Arbogast, the private investigator, is stabbed at the top of the stairs in the Bates house in the film version, not razor-slashed at the front door as in Bloch's novel. These changes were all made to increase suspense, as well as to enable the use of camera angles that would hide the true identity of "Mrs. Bates." If Marion had been decapitated, as in the novel, it would undoubtedly have made the sequence too gruesome and lessened its cinematic possibilities.

In spite of the fact that Hitchcock's film version follows Bloch's novel almost exactly and that Joseph Stefano's screenplay does not improve that much on the characterizations or far-fetched psychology of the piece, Bloch's book has invariably been belittled and scorned by admirers of the movie. This is because *Psycho*, the novel, is an adroit and compelling little melodrama, but nothing more. Certainly the fact that the movie version was made by an already famous and well-established master of suspense (whereas the novel was written by a man who is now only marginally more famous to the general public than he was then) had something to do with the movie's impact. But Hitchcock's movie challenged and played around with existing (in its case, cinematic) conventions in a way that the novel did not. For instance, in the novel the shower scene is tossed off in a few clever sentences, the actual murder in one line. No literary precedents were shattered. The shower sequence in the film shattered a great many precedents.

The plot of *Psycho* is as follows: Instead of depositing a client's money in the bank, Marion Crane (Janet Leigh) puts it in a suitcase and takes off for the town of Fairvale, determined to use the money to start a new life with her lover, store owner Sam Loomis (John Gavin), who hasn't been able to marry her because of

The money that sets *Psycho*'s story in motion. How can Marion resist?

expensive alimony payments. Marion loses her way in the rain and stops to spend the night at an isolated motel run by the shy, stammering Norman Bates, who tells her about his dreary life caring for his senile old mother. Bolstered by things Norman has said, she decides to return the money in the morning and see if she can rectify her error.

Before she can do so she is stabbed to death, apparently by the crazed old mother, while taking a shower. Lila (Vera Miles), Marion's sister, goes to Fairvale to talk to Sam about Marion's disappearance. She is followed by a private investigator named Arbogast (Martin Balsam). Arbogast is killed when he goes to talk to Norman's mother, and Lila and Sam check into the motel to continue the investigation. Lila is almost killed by Mrs. Bates—who turns out to be Norman, wearing an old dress and cheap wig, assuming the personality of his long-dead mother—but is rescued at the last minute by Loomis. Norman is put away.

Hitchcock was working on his show, *Alfred Hitchcock Presents*, at the time *Psycho*

Alfred Hitchcock on the set of *Psycho*, with his wife, Alma (sitting), and daughter, Pat, who appears in the film.

was filmed, and used his TV crew to shoot the movie quickly and economically. At first he wasn't confident about the picture and considered cutting out the gory parts and showing it on his program. He was, happily, convinced to do otherwise. Before he could have copies of the picture run off and shipped to theaters, his wife Alma pointed out that Janet Leigh could be seen swallowing, according to some sources, or blinking, according to others, when she was supposed to be dead, so Hitchcock had to fix that first before proceeding.

When the film opened on June 17, 1960, absolutely no one was permitted into the moviehouse once the showing had begun, at Alfred Hitchcock's personal insistence. This unprecedented policy, which had formerly only been applied to the legitimate theater, was upheld by most theater managers and tolerated by audiences, though in some states, such as Minnesota, small-town exhibitors were afraid they would lose customers and refused to enforce it.

Alfred Hitchcock goes over some finer points of wardrobe with Janet Leigh.

Psycho also started another precedent in that the film began playing at neighborhood theaters in the outer boroughs of New York while continuing to run at first-run theaters in Manhattan. Even *Psycho*'s trailer broke new ground in that not a single shot from the film was used. Instead, Hitchcock took the viewers on a tour of the set, stopping to comment on the grisly slayings that occur as he arrives at each murder's location. (There is a quick shot of a woman screaming in a shower, but it's not Janet Leigh.)

The critical reaction to *Psycho* was extremely mixed. In London it received almost exclusively negative reviews. Some felt it was because the critics were denied the opportunity to attend preview showings by Paramount Pictures and had to see the film at the theater, where it was showing at special times. They gave *Psycho* and Hitchcock a terrible drubbing, calling the picture "laughable," "boring," "Hitchcock's worst film," and damning it for being in the worst possible taste. One went so far as to say: "*Psycho* is more miserable than the most miserable peepshow I have ever seen, and far more awful and suggestive than any pornographic film I have ever seen." Kenneth Tynan later wrote in the *London Observer* that Psycho "was more comprehensively slaughtered by the critics than any other film of merit in modern times."

Several American reviewers commented on what they felt was the slow pace of the film. "A defect in the picture as a whole is that it takes too long to knife the blonde," wrote Paul V. Beckley in the *New York Herald Tribune*, adding, "I find it rather difficult to be amused at the forms insanity may take." Many of his colleagues also found the film psychologically dubious, if not ridiculous. They felt that *Psycho* was not typical Hitchcock, and indeed it was a change of pace for the prolific director.

There were some critics of the period, however, who recognized that *Psycho* was no ordinary thriller. Archer Winsten of the *New York Post* wrote: "As thrillers go, this is a good one because it uses the master's theories so effectively, and it is more than merely that, because it presents real aspects of a real world and then crumbles them slowly as you, transfixed, watch." And Andrew Sarris wrote in the *Village Voice*: "*Psycho* should be seen at least three times by any discerning film-goer, the first time for the sheer terror of the experience . . . ; the second time for the macabre comedy inherent in the conception of the film; and the third for all the hidden meanings and symbols lurking beneath the surface of the first American movie since *Touch of Evil* to stand in the same creative rank as the great European films."

Public interest in Hitchcock's film was high, as the movie did record-breaking business wherever it was showing, with long lines of anxious, curious ticket buyers all too willing to arrive on time so as not to be refused admittance. Though audiences seemed to find the movie suspenseful, scary, and enjoyable,

A provocative publicity poster of Janet Leigh for *Psycho*.

by no means was everyone so enamored. *The New York Times* published several thought-provoking letters pro-and-con which served as a barometer of public opinion across the country. The controversy started when one correspondent wrote in to express his "despair, horror and anger" over the picture.

There were a variety of responses to the letter. Though it was generally agreed that *Psycho* should be off-limits to impressionable youngsters, one man felt that the film was a "macabre joke" and "brilliant Gothic shocker" which adults could certainly enjoy. Another correspondent felt that the picture was deliberately constructed to pander to the audience's worst instincts. One man even suggested that perhaps it was time to employ more stringent standards of movie censorship before filmmakers could go any further. Conversely, it was pointed out that people were hypocritical to see a picture they knew was a murder mystery and then object when presented with the very murder they had come to see. Still, the more hysterical correspondents were convinced that Hitchcock's film was a blueprint for slaughter, and that maniacs across the country would be inspired to butcher victims once they saw it.

A couple of months after *Psycho* opened, some of the fears of the public seemed justified when the *New York Herald Tribune* ran this headline in their September 7, 1960 edition: ADMITS SLAYING THREE WOMEN, ONE AFTER SEEING *Psycho*. A 29-year-old optical worker was arrested in Hollywood during a purse-snatching attempt. He told police that he had killed a woman after taking her to see *Psycho*. He also said he had strangled at least two other older women. However, the suspect admitted that he could get these "urges to kill" at any time, and that, while *Psycho* had made an "impact" on him, he didn't believe it had much to do with his subsequent actions.

Another slaying indirectly connected to *Psycho* was that of Valerie Percy, 21-year-old daughter of Charles H. Percy, the Republican senatorial candidate for Illinois, who was stabbed to death in Chicago in September 1966. The CBS network decided to postpone the first scheduled TV showing of *Psycho* (on the prime-time *Friday Night at the Movies* of September 23, 1966) to avoid a tasteless correlation. CBS planned to reschedule the film but instead decided it simply wasn't right for TV audiences after the public and many CBS affiliates complained.

Psycho was finally shown on television by an ABC affiliate, WABC-TV (channel seven) in New York on June 24, 1967, at 11:30 in the evening. The shower murder was trimmed. Said a channel seven spokesman: "We don't feel we will destroy the dramatic content of the film if there are only ten stabbings in the shower rather than . . . thirty." Nowadays, *Psycho* is shown regularly at all hours all over the country, including showings in the afternoon, with the shower murder more or less intact.

That famous shower murder sequence, as Donald Spoto puts it in his book *The Dark Side of Genius: The Life of Alfred Hitchcock*, "changed the course of Hollywood history" and "has evoked more study, elicited more comment, and generated more shot-for-shot analysis from a technical viewpoint than any other in the history of the cinema."[3]

The violence of the shower murder elicited much response, including outrage.

"You had better have a pretty strong stomach and be prepared for a couple of grisly shocks when you go to see Alfred Hitchcock's *Psycho*, which a great many people are sure to do," wrote Bosley Crowther in *The New York Times*. "For Mr. Hitchcock, an old hand at frightening people, comes at you with a club in this frankly intended bloodcurdler." The shower murder was labeled by one of the *London Observer*'s critics "one of the most disgusting murders in all screen history. It takes place in a bathroom and involves a great deal of swabbing of the tiles and flushings of the lavatory. It might be described with fairness as plug-ugly, although I'm told that our British Board of Film Censors has expunged a lot of blood." However, the shower murder wasn't even mentioned by several reviewers, who'd been told not to give away too many of the picture's surprises or plot details.

The shower murder lasts for about forty-five seconds and consists of dozens of shots of a flashing knife intercut with Janet Leigh's horrified, anguished reactions. The knife is never shown actually penetrating the victim's body. Bernard Herrmann's stunning music expertly complements the action. The shot of the dark intruder seen through the shower curtain as he sneaks up behind Leigh is one of the most terrifying in the history of the movies.

There have always been two basic trends of thought concerning this sequence. One camp maintains that the sequence is simply brutal and obscene, a long, clinical death scene that records each blow and dying gasp of the victim and allows the audience to even gaze at her corpse for an extended period of time after the final stab is delivered. The other camp argues, as did Hitchcock, that the scene is not especially graphic (particularly when compared to the shockers of the 1980's!) and does not so much present a realistic, detailed butchershop sequence as an impressionistic flurry of quick, jangled shots that portray the confusion and horror of the victim. The audience does not dispassionately observe the murder; it becomes both victim and abuser, transformed by the sheer cinematic virtuosity of the undeniably rousing and exciting sequence. *Psycho* is clearly entertainment, not a documentary on murder.

However Hitchcock intended it, the scene goes beyond charnel-house voyeurism. It instills in the audience a sense of futility and waste. The horror and tragedy of a sudden, pointless death is vividly made apparent. The comparative silence at the end of the scene, when the music and Marion's screams have stopped and all that can be heard is the running shower and the gurgling of the drain, is the sound of the dreadful void that comes at the end of someone's life. The shot of the blood and water spiraling into the drain dissolves into a shot of the camera spiraling around Janet Leigh's dead, vacant eye. Marion Crane's senseless death is more pathetic with each viewing.

It is lucky, however, that Hitchcock's reputation doesn't rest solely on this remarkable and infamous sequence, for it has come to light that designer Saul Bass may have had more to do with it than Hitchcock did. Hitchcock did admit, in his famous interview with the late Francois Truffaut, that, besides designing the main titles, Bass did some layouts for the scene when the detective is murdered on the staircase. After the early part of the sequence was filmed, however, Hitchcock realized it didn't work and reshot it.[4] Then an interview with Bass was published in *American Cinematographer* (March 1977), wherein Bass claimed that he had actually planned and directed the shower sequence (at Hitchcock's request). A storyboard that Bass drew for the segment was also published along with the interview. In Spoto's book, Janet Leigh is quoted as saying that this was essentially the truth. Hitchcock stuck to Bass' storyboard, but did add a couple shots of his own. (In *Psycho*'s opening credits Bass is billed as both "Title Designer" and "Pictorial Consultant.")

However accurate the story of Bass' involvement is, it doesn't change the fact that *Psycho* is a fine picture and that Hitchcock is an excellent director. *Psycho*, like any other movie, may be guided and shaped by one individual (in this case, Hitchcock), but that doesn't mean that it is not the product of a great many talented people. Bass' opening title designs are excellent. Bernard Herrmann's score is the richest and most evocative ever written for a thriller (still imitated by the late Mr. Herrmann's inferiors). The art direction by Joseph Hurley and Robert Clatworthy is superb. Most of the performances are adroit and compelling.

In spite of its low-budget, black-and-white filming, *Psycho* is not some cheap, poorly made, slapdash piece of junk hastily thrown together without rhyme or reason. There is a point and purpose to each shot, unlike the shoddy subsequent horror products that merely plod along from one murder to the next without any style, thought, or personal vision. The picture is full of wonderful touches and moments that are not immediately noticed upon first or even fourth viewing. These include the interesting detail of the mother's room (the indentation of her body is still on the mattress), the curious objects in Norman's bedroom, and the mother's skull superimposed over the last shot of Norman's face as he sits calmly in the stationhouse.

The shot of Janet Leigh's approach to the Bates Motel is remarkably sinister. The neon sign of the motel is at first just a glare of hazy white light all but hidden by the windshield wipers and the rain pouring down over the glass. Normally music is used in horror films to tell the audience to "watch out!"—that something is up. The absence of music in this sequence makes the point more effectively. The clattering, metric sound of the windshield wiper is like an anticipatory drum roll. There is a consistently ominous tension to the movie that carries through the slow spots. The film's dark, oppressive pessimism is perfectly captured in the scene when Marion checks into the motel and learns that she is only fifteen miles from her destination. The whole murder could have been avoided if she'd only kept driving; she is a victim of the vagaries of fate.

Joseph Stefano has supplied some sophisticated dialogue that lifts the characters somewhat above the one-dimensional level some critics perceive them

Marion (Janet Leigh) checks into the Bates Motel, while Norman (Anthony Perkins) watches.

as being on. Even when they border on being pretentious, the lines have a certain poetic flair. For instance, Norman's speech to Marion as he watches her eat her sandwich: "I think that we're all in our private traps, clamped in them. And none of us can ever get out. We scratch and claw, but only at the air, only at each other. And for all of it, we never budge an inch." Also, Norman's remarks about his mother's mental condition and the idea of putting her in a madhouse are both frightening and poignant, particularly in that he's talking about himself.

Other talky sequences are enlivened by wonderful acting. Anthony Perkins is at his best when he shares the spotlight with that fine actor, Martin Balsam. The sharp pacing and staccato delivery of the dialogue in the scene when Arbogast questions Bates about Marion Crane and catches him in several contradictions makes it one of the best-played sequences in the movie.

Although the shower murder has received most of the attention, Arbogast's murder on the staircase is also inventively staged, cleverly designed to hide the identity of the killer by filming the action from high overhead. It is not only these flamboyant sequences that are cinematic. For example, when Marion is awakened by a policeman after falling asleep in her car on the side of the road, Hitchcock heightens her confusion and paranoia by immediately cutting to a huge close up of the policeman's stony face staring in through the window. The many subjective shots in the film put the audience in the place of the characters and add to the suspense.

In spite of its superior quality, there are flaws in *Psycho*. Janet Leigh is perhaps too limited an actress to fully convey Marion's desperation, frustration, and impulsiveness. Vera Miles is a good actress, but John Gavin is a bit wooden. Neither of them react with any particular grief or shock when Marion's death, which they have feared throughout the movie, is confirmed at the end of the picture, as much a directorial mistake as theirs.

There are script contrivances, such as the scene when Marion subtracts on a piece of paper the money she's spent from the stolen $40,000. While the scene is not entirely unrealistic (it's almost a symbolic gesture on Marion's part), and is necessary in that Vera Miles must later find part of that paper in the toilet, it's still hard to believe that Marion couldn't simply have subtracted the easy figures in her head.

The pace of the picture is too slow at times (at least in subsequent viewings). For instance, why didn't Hitchcock break up the static scene when Arbogast calls Lila from a phone booth, after he has spoken to Norman, with a reaction shot or two of Lila on the other end of the line? Hitchcock himself felt that the scenes when Lila and Sam talk to the police were rather dull.

For all its good points, *Psycho* never really penetrates below a certain surfacy scare level in dealing with its themes and characters. It is an artistic film because

Martin Balsam, as the private investigator, asks Norman Bates too many questions in this very-well-acted scene from *Psycho*.

of its technique, not because of its content, which is one reason why the film has always garnered mixed reactions and why many of its greatest admirers are also critical of it.

In the years since 1960, *Psycho* has been subjected to the most intensive scrutiny and (over) analysis. Hitchcock meant it to be taken simply as a fun, escapist horror film, but some critics insist that *Psycho* is a film of deep meaning and profound intent. Such books as *Hitchcock's Films* by Robin Wood,[5] and *Hitchcock—The Murderous Gaze* by William Rothman,[6] among others, subject the picture to every possible (and often fascinating) interpretation, going over each scene and every shot to probe for layers of meaning. The latter book devotes nearly one hundred pages to such exhaustive analysis.

While *Psycho* is not necessarily a film totally devoid of complexity, it is not—and was never meant to be—a heavy, meaningful drama of insightful characterization and awesome consequence. As far as Hitchcock was concerned, *Psycho* was a cinematic exercise, an experiment in storytelling that works marvelously and is rich and inventive on that level. To ascribe to it deeper, suspect motives and meanings is tantamount to stripping it of its genuine contribution and significance.

Critics also make a mistake in harping on Hitchcock's "brilliance" and "daring" in killing off his heroine a third of the way into his film. True, Kenneth Tynan did note that in *Psycho* "for the first time in movie history, the heroine—with whom we have been encouraged to identify—has actually been murdered." Yet this basic idea was lifted from Robert Bloch's novel.

Although *Psycho*'s shock value has undoubtedly been diminished by time and the cinema's increasing preoccupation with graphic bloodshed, it still works very well for contemporary audiences who have never seen the picture before. Concentrating on the stolen $40,000, 1985 audiences still get sidetracked by the suspenseful early scenes—Marion's encounter with the policeman and her switching of automobiles—as Hitchcock intended. When Norman puts the car with Marion's body in it into the swamp, audiences still gasp and chuckle when it stops sinking for a moment—as Hitchcock intended. While the shower murder itself may have lost its power to repulse, a breathless current nevertheless runs through the audience when Janet Leigh turns on the water and that figure starts to creep up behind her. Why does *Psycho* need profound implications when twenty-five years later it still does what it was always intended to do?

Psycho was a highly profitable motion picture. By 1961 *Time* magazine reported that it had already returned "the highest percentage of profit in film history—$14,000,000 on a $780,000 investment." CBS had paid $800,000, the cost of the film, for just two TV showings that it never even ran. There was no doubt that in financial terms *Psycho* was a smashing success, one reason why there have been so many imitations, indeed, why a whole new type of picture was created. Not only did Alfred Hitchcock prove that he could make a better horror film, but the success of *Psycho* ensured that the genre would flourish for many years to come.

The film has had other long-lasting effects. Andrew Sarris wrote, back in 1960, that "such divergent American institutions as motherhood and motels will never seem quite the same again," and added, twenty-one years later: "I cannot deny that Hitchcock opened some sort of Pandora's box with *Psycho*, and that *Dressed to Kill* and *The Fan*, along with a flock of other variably poisonous entertainments, have flown out of this box, often with Pandora as a murderous male in drag."

Even today some people get a chill of memory when they drive up to a small motel on an isolated highway, or step into the shower naked and vulnerable. There have been literally dozens of articles and hundreds of book pages devoted to the film, and *Psycho* was one of the few comparatively recent films to be

Tony Perkins poses with one of Norman's stuffed birds in this publicity shot.

included in The Film Classics Library, a series of books that feature blow ups of every single still of important motion pictures.[7] Several directors have been influenced by the picture and tried to make their own versions or "homages." William Castle, Brian De Palma, and dozens of lesser known filmmakers are on the list. Even the contemporary "mad slasher" films, such as *Halloween* and *Friday the 13th*, which today's teenagers are more familiar with and which shamelessly rip off one another, are cut from the same cloth as *Psycho*, though in infinitely inferior fashion. Today, *Psycho* is more admired by the critical establishment than it was when first released. Many critics number it among the finest pictures ever made.

Hitchcock, who died in 1980, made a number of films after *Psycho*, one of which was a certified bomb (*Topaz*/1969), one an unqualified success (*Frenzy*/ 1972), and the rest of which received mixed reactions. (These films, including *Marnie* (1964) and *Torn Curtain* (1966), were underrated at the time, and are only now coming into their own.) *The Birds* (1963) and *Frenzy* are the only two that can legitimately be classified as shockers, and they are discussed in the following chapter. Universal, which now owns the rights to *Psycho* after acquiring them from Paramount, made a sequel, *Psycho Two*, in 1983. It, too, is discussed in Chapter Three.

Anthony Perkins made a great many films after *Psycho*, most of which were not retreads of his Norman Bates role (contrary to popular opinion), but Hitchcock's film is the one for which he is best remembered. He admitted on *Late Night with David Letterman* in 1984 that his constant identification with the role used to bother him, but no more. Perkins reprised the role in *Psycho Two*. Many feel that Perkins' highwater mark was when he co-starred with Ingrid Bergman a year after *Psycho* in *Goodbye Again* (1961), in which he gives an affecting performance as an impetuous and lonely fellow who has an affair with a middle-aged woman. He recently played another "wacko" role in Ken Russell's *Crimes of Passion* (1984).

In the summer of 1985 Perkins made *Psycho Three* in Hollywood, serving as both director and star. Reportedly, this latest installment of the Norman Bates saga will bring Perkins face to face with a Marion Crane lookalike (Diana Scarwid) and provide another grisly shower encounter.

The film output of Janet Leigh, Vera Miles, and John Gavin has been relatively undistinguished since 1960, with none of their subsequent films or appearances having the impact of *Psycho*. John Gavin is now the U.S. Ambassador to Mexico. Martin Balsam remains one of the screen's finest character actors, and appeared with Carroll O'Connor for a season or two of *Archie Bunker's Place*.

Speaking of TV stars, an uncredited extra at the end of *Psycho* who stands mutely outside the door to the room where the now totally psychotic Norman Bates has been incarcerated is none other than Ted Knight, who made a strong comedic impression playing anchorman Ted Baxter for seven years on *The Mary Tyler Moore Show*.

THE SINCEREST FORM OF FLATTERY

An entire book could be devoted to movies that are partial or complete imitations of *Psycho*. There's hardly a film or director in the shock/suspense field who has not been influenced by the picture. *Psycho* helped open up more graphic approaches to violence and sexuality, and, just as important, the link between the two. It also inspired a great many films that dealt with lurid aspects of multiple-personality disorder, psychopathology, and transvestism. Even specific scenes, particularly the shower murder, were copied from *Psycho*.

Psycho took great pains to make it clear that Norman Bates was not necessarily a transvestite. Norman did not dress up as a woman for sexual thrills as such; he dressed up, in effect, to keep his mother alive. In spite of this distinction, a great many of *Psycho*'s imitators feature killers who are transvestites or transsexuals. Most of these films simply exploit their subject matter, and worse, make it seem as if anyone who has an unusual sexual bent also has to be unbalanced and homicidal.

Because of the public's tendency to confuse transvestism with homosexuality, many people have assumed that Norman Bates was gay. Actually, Norman—or his "mother" persona—stabbed women because he was attracted to them. Robert Bloch confirmed Bates' heterosexual preferences in his novel *Psycho Two*.

The shower murder was so bold and unprecedented in its shock value that filmmakers have been fascinated by it ever since. It has come in for more than its share of imitations, parodies, and homages, even in films that are not of the genre.

Sometimes the shower scene is spoofed for comic effect. In Mel Brooks' Hitchcock parody, *High Anxiety* (1977), the director-actor takes a shower in his hotel room. Brooks expertly recreates the opening shots of *Psycho*'s shower scene. But when the curtain is drawn aside and a hand thrusts toward the naked comedian, it turns out only to be the bellboy holding a newspaper. In *Fade to*

Jean Arless threatens Eugenie Leontovich (in silhouette) with a knife in William Castle's *Psycho* rip-off, *Homicidal*.

Black (1980), the maniacal protagonist sneaks up on a showering beauty and playfully lunges at her with a pen that drips black ink. Rolled up sheet music takes the place of a butcher knife in Brian De Palma's *Phantom of the Paradise* (1974). The shower scene was even spoofed on magician David Copperfield's seventh TV show, in March 1985, when an elaborate tribute to *Psycho* was capped with Copperfield making Angie Dickinson disappear from behind a shower curtain!

Often the girl-in-the-shower bit is merely a suspense tease, an ominous scene that turns out to be a red herring, with the "attacker" unmasked as a playful sibling or the "victim's" amorous boyfriend. This sort of thing occurs in *The Funhouse, Night School, Mean Season*, and many others. Brian De Palma's *Dressed to Kill* (1980) has two scary shower scenes. No one gets stabbed in either, but the audience thinks it's going to happen. William Castle tried a variation in *I Saw What You Did* (1965). And there have been countless terror films in which ladies step underneath a showerhead (showing much more of their breasts than Janet

Leigh ever did or was allowed) for a few tense seconds, only to get out moments later and go about their business unharmed. In some pictures people are actually murdered while taking a shower, but these scenes are so perfunctorily handled that it's hard to conceive of them as being influenced by *Psycho* beyond the setting of the murder. Jason Vorhees crushes the head of a showering male victim in *Friday the 13th: The Final Chapter*. A woman is scalded to death in her shower in *Psychic Killer*. And another showering beauty is punctured by a pitchfork in *The Prowler*. And these are just a few from a long list.

Psycho also inspired a number of films that were merely blatant copies of it. The early to mid-sixties yielded a wealth of movies that were directly influenced by the box-office success of Hitchcock's thriller.

The first and, arguably, best of these is *Homicidal*, which the late director William Castle brought out in July 1961, a little over a year after *Psycho*'s release. In his autobiography, *Step Right Up! I'm Gonna Scare the Pants Off America*,[8] the prolific producer/director makes no mention of any influence that *Psycho*'s plot or style may have had on him. He does, however, admit that Hitchcock's gimmick of admitting no one into theaters after the film had started inspired him to come up with a better one for *Homicidal*. Castle was the undisputed King of the Gimmicks, coming up with bizarre ideas to help publicize each of his pictures. He dangled a skeleton over the heads of the audience during showings of *House on Haunted Hill*, and wired selected seats to give mild shocks to patrons who were watching *The Tingler*!

The gimmick for *Homicidal* was a "fright break," which occurred only moments before the end of the picture. "Cowards" could leave the theater during this brief intermission and ask for their money back. In a special test preview of the film, hundreds of members of the audience did just that. Castle finally realized that most people had stayed twice: once to see the picture and a second time just to get the refund! Castle countered this by having different colored tickets issued for each performance.

Homicidal is a shameless imitation of *Psycho*. Even screenwriter Robb White, who fashioned the story from Castle's suggested plot elements, told *Fangoria* interviewer John Wooley that when he finally got around to seeing *Psycho* he was embarrassed to realize *Homicidal* was just Castle's copy of it. Castle took elements of Hitchcock's film, distorted and enlarged them into an incredible script about a crazed female transvestite (this time the real thing, unlike Norman Bates who was simply trying to keep the memory of his mother alive), who commits gruesome murders in order to claim his/her inheritance. At least the situations in *Psycho*, inspired by real life events, seemed reasonable enough in their horrific context. *Homicidal*'s exaggerated style and screenplay made it seem as if its events were unfolding in some alternate dimension. In spite of this, *Homicidal* is Castle's highwater mark. Though he made other entertaining pictures, such as *Thirteen Ghosts* (1960), none were ever as effective as his elaborate *Psycho* rip-off.

The plot hinges on the gimmick of a girl being raised as a boy since birth (the reverse idea has been used in several subsequent films, such as 1973's *Reflection of Fear*). Castle interviewed a number of men for the part, but settled on actress Joan Marshall, whose stage name he changed to Jean Arless, to play the dual role. Except for noticeable dubbing when she is dressed as her other half, Warren, the trick works surprisingly well, and the makeup is effective. A viewer who has been clued in to the sex switch can spot it by paying careful attention, but back in 1961 most viewers were fooled. Male actors have performed in drag countless times, but the opposite was and still is infrequent. Arless makes a fairly convincing man, and dressed as her real, feminine self makes a cold and nasty-looking murderer.

Homicidal's plot twist: Look closely—the "guy" on the right is really a woman (Jean Arless).

Jean Arless gets ready to butcher the old woman who knows her deadly secret in *Homicidal*.

Homicidal is by no means in the league of *Psycho*. It is strident and frequently ridiculous, but it does have some nice visual shocks, as well as a few moments of tension. Like *Psycho*, the film contains two flamboyant murder scenes. Arless checks into a hotel and gets a handsome bellboy to agree to marry her in exchange for some cash. But when they're standing before the portly justice of the peace, Arless pulls out a butcher knife and stabs the magistrate repeatedly in the belly, drawing lots and lots of blood. Castle figured that if he couldn't recreate the technical proficiency of Hitchcock's shower murder, he could at least top Hitchcock by making *Homicidal*'s first murder scene much gorier than *Psycho*'s.

The second murder scene is greatly abetted by the performance of distinguished stage actress Eugenie Leontovich, who plays an elderly crippled mute doomed to die before she can somehow communicate Arless's deadly secret. Aware that she is in mortal danger, Leontovich desperately tries to alert a visitor to her dilemma, but is unable to make him understand what is agitating her. The scene borders on black comedy.

Arless gets her knife sharpened by a man who stops by, then goes back into the house, where she advances on Leontovich. The terrified mute tries to escape by getting into the motorized chair she uses to go up and down the staircase. Later, when heroine Patricia Breslin goes into the house at the end of the picture, Leontovich's shadow looms on the wall. Her head nods forward, and *keeps on tipping*, until it rolls off completely. Castle was shrewd enough to realize that there is something particularly nasty about decapitation, and knew he could go Hitchcock one better by including the beheading that Hitchcock had omitted from his film version of *Psycho*.

Critical reaction to *Homicidal* was mixed. *The New York Times* bemoaned the fact that the film was ever made, feeling that the "venerable Eugenie Leontovich, at least, would have been spared [the] public humiliation of being seen in such trash, and a blonde called Jean Arless could have avoided the season's most embarrassing film debut." On the other hand, *Time* magazine admitted that *Homicidal* "was obviously made in imitation of Hitchcock's thriller," but then added: "Just as obviously it surpasses its model in structure, suspense and sheer nervous drive."

This is a surprising opinion because it ignores the simple fact that Hitchcock was the original artist and Castle the hack imitator.

Both films feature killers who cross-dress, and were made at a time when the only real or imagined transvestites in films were absurd comedic figures. Aside from Edward D. Wood, Jr.'s campy *Glen or Glenda?* (1953), aspects of transvestism were simply not explored in motion pictures. Both films have violent stabbing sequences that are unexpected to the uninitiated, and also have a second, less violent murder that occurs on a staircase. Both films flagrantly link sexual disturbances and identity confusion with violence and psychosis. Castle made *Homicidal* only because *Psycho* was so successful.

Most critics were moderate. They found only amusement in the whole concept and production. Paul V. Beckley in the *New York Herald Tribune* wrote: "Castle's shock effects are not so much of the weird or 'horror' as of the gruesome or blood-on-the-cummerbund variety. He dotes on the clunking sounds that accompany a half dozen knife thrusts . . . I know some may assert that a taste for tumbling heads bespeaks an unsavory yen for the sadistic, but I suspect that both Castle and his particular audiences look on it as a rather grim form of comedy, an appeal to the sense of the grotesque."

Homicidal has made little impact on the film scene, though people do occasionally confuse it with *Psycho*. In fact, soul singer James Brown told Alfred Hitchcock how much he enjoyed his *Homicidal* on a talk show. (Hitchcock gave him a glance that could have withered steel.) *Homicidal* remains a clever, amusing, somewhat scary minor melodrama, but it's not the masterpiece-of-its-kind that *Psycho* is.

Somewhat pathetically, Castle spent the rest of his career trying to become a clone of Alfred Hitchcock. He appeared in his own films (including a silly prologue to *Homicidal*), hired Robert Bloch to write the screenplay for his *Strait-Jacket* (with Joan Crawford), and even filmed a dismal shower murder of his own in *I Saw What You Did*. Castle undeniably had showmanship, but he lacked the raw talent he needed to emulate the man whose work he so admired and whose professional reputation he so coveted. Castle later produced such well-received pictures as Roman Polanski's screen version of Ira Levin's *Rosemary's Baby*. Sadly, with just one picture, Hitchcock was able to take the kind of film Castle specialized in and do it much better than Castle ever could, something that must have gnawed at Castle's insides until the grave.

Other directors of the sixties tried to do their own versions of *Psycho*, but none were as obsessed as Castle. One of the early films directed by Francis Ford Coppola (who later turned out such famous films as *The Godfather*, *Godfather, Part II*, and *Apocalypse Now*), was *Dementia 13* (a.k.a. *The Haunted and the Hunted*/1963), a thriller set in an Irish castle. The plot revolves around a greedy wife who becomes the victim of an axe murderer, with the other members of her batty family as the suspects. A few nice gruesome moments are all there is to recommend in this rather idiotic production, which one critic said "will doubtless produce a few spasms of disgust," while another noted "you'll be happy to know that when that deadly [axe] comes crashing down, blood spurts and heads actually roll." *Dementia 13* imitates *Psycho* by killing off a major character in a rousing murder scene about a third of the way into the running time, yet unsuccessfully attempts to recreate the tense, vivid atmosphere of Hitchcock's picture.

But *Dementia 13* was lauded as a masterpiece compared to the critical reception given *Psychomania* (1964), about a maniac on the loose in a small-town campus. Jay Carr in the *New York Post* wrote "No fewer than 71—count 'em—71 clichés assault the eye and ear in *Psychomania*." Howard Thompson in *The New York Times* said "The murders are a poor man's reprise of Mr. Hitchcock's famous shower scene in *Psycho*;" and the *New York Daily News* bellowed: "With the sick feeding on the sick, meaning the peddlers and purchasers of pornographia, the movie industry becomes increasingly gangrenous. Among recent dregs of the trade is *Psychomania*, once labeled *Sexomania*." Despite these virulent opinions, *Psychomania* is a creditable if unenthusiastic effort, with a scary final encounter in a deserted house and a surprise twist ending. The script, however, is mediocre, and director Richard Hilliard's talent doesn't quite match his ambition.

This victim of the raging *Psychopath* looks pretty "tired."

Although the screenplay for the movie version of his novel *Psycho* was written by Joseph Stefano, Robert Bloch found his talents as screenwriter much in demand in Hollywood due to his connection with Hitchcock's thriller. His work has always been uneven, often merely lackluster retreads involving psychopaths and weird old ladies, but occasionally he comes up with an imaginative, engaging variation. Such a happy occasion was his script for *The Couch* (1962), an odd little horror film about a psycho (Grant Williams) who kills perfect strangers at seven P.M. every evening. Bloch's script contains the usual dime-store psychology, but works ingeniously on all other levels: the synchronism, the murders them-selves—which are more grotesque because of the anonymity of the victims—and the brilliance of the denouement, which reveals the motive for the bizarre killings. While there are plenty of weak spots to the production, *The Couch* is a surprisingly good thriller with a very disquieting atmosphere. Owen Crump's direction isn't bad and there are more than enough effective touches and suspenseful moments.

Bloch also wrote the screenplay for the British thriller, *The Psychopath* (1966), about a group of friends who get together weekly to play chamber music. One by one they become murder victims. Small dolls dressed as the victims are left at the scenes of the crimes. These slayings are tied in to Mrs. Von Sturm (Margaret Johnston), a German widow who is confined to a wheelchair and surrounds herself with dozens of dolls. The film received mixed notices. Several critics wondered how on earth the killer could possibly know beforehand what clothes the victims would be wearing when she kills them, and have time yet to sew up tiny little imitations of their outfits. *The Psychopath*, directed by Freddie Francis, was generally considered a decent enough thriller, but it did nothing to make anyone forget *Psycho*.

Critics wondered: How does *The Psychopath* know beforehand what clothes her victims would be wearing?

In 1965 director Roman Polanski decided to make a film that would delve deeper into the psychotic mentality, rather than simply use it as a vehicle for murder. *Repulsion* is about a manicurist (Catherine Deneuve) who has trouble dealing with men, the very male presence, in fact. She is slowly cracking up, becoming withdrawn and experiencing frightening hallucinations. She kills her puzzled boyfriend, then slashes her landlord to death with a straight razor. *Repulsion* is a complex film that is clearly the work of a talented filmmaker, and has several inventive scenes, such as when the heroine accidentally nips and bloodies the finger of a matron whose nails she is working on. The murder sequences are poorly handled, however. They seem to have been filmed with a shaky hand-held camera, and lack fluidity. The boppy jazz score that backs up the murders is completely inappropriate. Still, *Repulsion* garnered a lot of attention for the director when it was released.

Polanski later teamed up with schlock-master William Castle when he directed Castle's production of *Rosemary's Baby* (1968). This adaptation of Ira Levin's novel of modern-day witchcraft is not entirely successful. While it effectively shows how lurking evil can hide behind the commonplace, it rarely attempts to be convincingly frightening. The film is further marred by the casting of overly familiar faces as the coven, some of whom are given campish roles to play. Polanski's direction is uneven, vividly bringing some sequences to life while undermining others. He went on to direct the controversial *Macbeth* (1971), a graphic reenactment of the play, which many felt was his way of achieving a catharsis over the bloody butchery of his wife, the late actress Sharon Tate, who was killed with several others by the crazed cultist Charles Manson.

There were other British chillers aside from *The Psychopath* that, despite unique storylines, tried to cash in on *Psycho*'s success. *Maniac* (1963), *Paranoiac* (1963), and *Hysteria* (1965), are three such attempts. *Paranoiac*, directed by Freddie Francis, concerns a young man who impersonates a long-lost heir and discovers weird things about a family in an English mansion, such as organ music in the middle of the night and an ugly clown who roams about with homicidal intentions. There are some eerie moments and interesting bits and a decent enough plot, plus an excellent performance from Oliver Reed as the protagonist's jealous sibling, but *Paranoiac* doesn't have the energy to match its insane histrionics. It got very mixed reviews upon its release, though Howard Thompson in *The New York Times* said: "This Freudian mishmash opens with devilish adroitness, and whips up considerable suspense and conviction," though he, too, thought it collapsed in the final quarter.

Hysteria, also directed by Freddie Francis, is about an American (Robert Webber) who survives a car wreck, but develops amnesia and starts hallucinating. He even sees the body of a woman in his bathtub. (This summons up in the

William Castle finally had a hit when he produced *Rosemary's Baby* (with John Cassavetes and Mia Farrow).

minds of the audience the image of Janet Leigh sprawled over the tub in *Psycho*.) His psychiatric bills are paid for by an unknown benefactor, who also sets him up in a beautiful penthouse apartment. It all turns out to be a plot to pin a murder rap on the hapless fellow.

Maniac, directed by Michael Carreras, is the most successful of the three. Kerwin Matthews is a vacationing painter who gets involved with a mother and her daughter at a small French inn. The girl's father had been put away after turning a blow torch on the man who raped her (the blow-torch murder occurs in a prologue sequence). His wife enlists Matthews in a scheme to break her husband out of prison, assuming that her husband has accepted the fact that she now loves Matthews. Audiences may not have had trouble guessing the first plot twist in Jimmy Sangster's clever screenplay, or even the second. But the final twist fooled everyone. *Maniac* is a superior suspense story with a fast pace, a good cast, and nice locations all adding to that terrific script. Carreras' direction, while above average for this kind of low-budget stuff, is not very stylish or especially memorable. What *Maniac* and most of the other films mentioned in this chapter needed was a director with the talent and originality of Alfred Hitchcock.

There were several other British and American chillers made during this period that tried to form an association with *Psycho* in the public's eye so that they, too, might break box-office records like *Psycho* did (and like no other horror film did before it). Often the only similarities these films had to *Psycho* (besides an abundance of psychopathic characters) was a catchy, creepy, one-word title that was ominous and easily remembered. *Trauma* and *Terrified*, two low-budget items made in 1962, are examples.

There were also many films made through the early sixties that were neither directly influenced by *Psycho* nor tried to come up with a similar one-word title,

The Collector is bored with butterflies and tries to pin down a female victim.

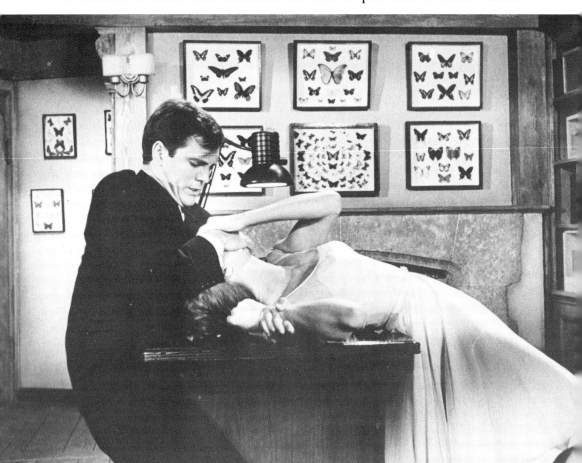

but which embraced themes that had been inspired by *Psycho*, or contained sequences that might not have been attempted had Hitchcock not first brought down the barriers. The success of *Psycho* also ensured that many unrelated horror properties were made, in the hope that the public was ready for a tidal wave of macabre and chilling film fare of a more intense and lurid nature than before. Horror movies, particularly of a supernatural nature, had always been successful at the box office, but after the phenomenal performance of *Psycho*, movies about psychotics in the troubled-but-attractive Norman Bates tradition were all the rage. Often that was the only similarity these films had to *Psycho*.

Surely the success of *Psycho* prompted a 1964 remake of *Night Must Fall*, the 1937 chiller about a charming male servant (and axe murderer) who moves into a household comprised of women and brings with him a hatbox that contains a human head. Albert Finney was a better-looking, more virile version of Norman Bates. Terence Stamp also played a charming whacko in William Wyler's controversial *The Collector* (1965), about a butterfly collector who kidnaps and imprisons a young woman, played by Samantha Eggar.

Other filmmakers figured that the only thing better than one beautiful woman being gruesomely murdered was a whole series of beautiful women being gruesomely murdered. The result was movies like *The Hypnotic Eye* (1960), in which women are hypnotized into disfiguring themselves in assorted painful ways. *Circus of Horrors* (1960) may have been released too soon after *Psycho* to have been influenced by it, but this rousing murder-under-the-big-top shocker was favorably compared to Hitchcock's classic by *The New York Times* reviewer and others.

Hitchcock himself tried to top the success of *Psycho* a couple of times. His very next film after *Psycho* was *The Birds* (1963), a splendidly cinematic story of our feathered friends massing together to attack a small seaside community in California. It remains one of Hitchcock's most accomplished works, with a host of superb, visually stunning sequences and special effects: the three successive shots of the dead man in the bedroom, ending with a close up of his face, with its gouged-out eyes; the crows on the monkey bars; the quick, frozen shots of Tippi Hedren and others watching the fire flash across the spilled stream of gasoline; the attack on the town, with a striking aerial shot of gulls descending as if attracted by the fire; the shots of Hedren in the phone booth and what she sees while inside it. The attack on Rod Taylor's house is effective, despite a near absence of birds, and the final attic attack—in which Hedren comes under a stabbing, well-edited assault from hundreds of panicking seagulls—is so exciting and well constructed that it's almost a reworking of the *Psycho* shower murder.

Hitchcock's *Frenzy* (1972) was advertised as a "masterpiece of shock," an attempt to create the kind of excitement that had developed over *Psycho*. After

The terrific advertisement for Alfred Hitchcock's *The Birds*.

Tippi Hedren is attacked by a crazed seagull in *The Birds*.

having directed several films that received lackluster critical reaction, Hitchcock found himself with his most well-received picture in years, with many reviewers applauding the "master of suspense"'s return to "top form." The film, while not really a masterpiece per se, is still far superior to most of the competition.

The plot concerns a man (Jon Finch) who is wrongly accused of a series of sex murders, and who must try to convince people of his innocence. Perhaps the best and most macabre scene occurs when the actual killer must retrieve damaging evidence (a stickpin) from the clenched fist of a naked victim he has thrown into the back of a potato truck. He climbs in back just as the truck begins to move and has great difficulty getting back the pin, finally having to break the woman's fingers to release it. The rape/strangulation of a woman who runs a dating service (which is analyzed fully in Chapter Four) is also memorable. There's a wonderful bit, as well, in which Hitchcock endows the simple act of walking up a flight of stairs with as much tension as when Martin Balsam walks up the stairs to his death in *Psycho*. *Frenzy* is absorbing, taut, and well worth seeing.

On the set of *Psycho Two* with Tony Perkins (right).

Vera Miles had better keep her mouth closed. *Psycho Two*'s killer is about to stick a spade in it.

Psycho Two is the ultimate *Psycho* imitation. It was made twenty-three years after the original. Anthony Perkins and Vera Miles reprised their roles and Richard Franklin is the director.

That same year, Robert Bloch's sequel to *Psycho*, also entitled *Psycho Two*, was published, but the storyline for his novel is completely different than the movie's. In Bloch's book, Bates escapes from the mental institution in which he is incarcerated by dressing up as a nun. Apparently he then heads out to Hollywood where they are filming a motion picture based on his life and times. There are a couple of murders, but it's revealed at the end that someone other than Norman is responsible.

In *Psycho Two*, the movie, Norman Bates is released from the insane asylum, much to the consternation of Lila Loomis. (In the intervening years Lila Crane has married her late sister's boyfriend, Sam Loomis, who has since died.) During the hearing, Lila protests the decision to release Norman Bates. Vera Miles plays her in such an agitated style, especially in contrast to Perkins' calm demeanor, that the audience sympathizes with Norman and takes Lila to be the villain. The audience identifies with Perkins during the film's early scenes, when he gets a job as a short-order cook, becomes friends with a sweet young woman (Meg Tilly), and tries to build a new life for himself in spite of grim reminders of the past. Lila Loomis' behavior also has to do with a plot twist revealed near the end of the picture.

Norman isn't going to have an easy time of it. Lila, who turns out to be Tilly's mother, is determined to see him back in the nuthouse, and has been dressing up as the late Mrs. Bates in an attempt to drive him crazy. Miles has a great grisly death scene, wherein someone shoves a spade into her mouth as she's digging up the clothes in the old fruit cellar and preparing to go into her "act."

The first half of *Psycho Two* isn't bad. Anthony Perkins is restrained and appealing, giving one of his better performances. Richard Franklin's direction is sharp, and the general look of the film is tight and handsome. There are a couple of well-handled murder scenes (of an obnoxious hotel manager and a young man fooling around in the basement) and a generous amount of suspense. The audience can't help but wonder if Norman has lost his mind again or if someone is persecuting him. In its second half, however, *Psycho Two* turns into something resembling a *Saturday Night Live* parody. Everything falls apart, the plot goes in several directions, and the script becomes a dribbling mess. Perkins is forced to ham it up dreadfully—some really embarrassing moments—as Norman begins to lose his mind, insisting that his "mother" is calling him on the telephone. Meg Tilly's performance goes from ingratiating to amateurish, as she gives all her lines the same monotonous delivery. The denouement is clever and amusing (if wildly contrived), but by that time the whole thing has become such a burlesque show that it hardly matters.

It turns out that Norman was adopted—Mrs. Bates was *not* his mother. His *real* mother, who has been close by all this time, has committed the latest batch of murders in order to "protect" her boy. After she sits down at the kitchen table to confess all to Norman, the by now thoroughly crazed fellow takes a shovel, bats "Ma" on the head with it, and kills her. Apparently, it's back to the nuthouse for Norman.

Psycho Two is still an entertaining film, far superior to most of the average "stalk and slash" offerings, with a lot of tense and spooky moments. It's a shame that Franklin and his associates couldn't have had a bit more reverence for the classic they were aping. Such wasted potential and talent turns *Psycho Two* into a mere freakshow instead of the true homage to a great film and filmmaker that it could and should have been.

But the saga of Norman Bates is not yet over. Perhaps *Psycho Three*, to be released in 1986, will be more on the mark.

CHAPTER FOUR

WOMEN AS VICTIMS

Why are women usually the victims in horror movies? Donald Spoto suggests, in his book on Hitchcock, that the violence against women in Hitchcock's *Psycho*, *The Birds*, and other films, may have been due to the director's resentment toward his leading ladies. But even in Bloch's novel, *Psycho*, it was a woman who took that fateful shower—a beautiful blonde woman—not a man.

There have been many documented cases of male mass murderers picking off a string of female victims, some of whose exploits have themselves been made into movies (*Jack the Ripper*, *The Boston Strangler*, *The Hollywood Hillside Strangler*). Occasionally, a maniac will kill both men and women (Son of Sam) or concentrate on male victims (John Wayne Gacy), but the vast majority of serial killers are men who hate and murder women. It follows suit, then, that filmmakers making movies about maniacal murderers would reflect the most prevalent situation in real life, and use young women as the victims.

Traditionally women have been thought of as physically weaker than men (an attitude that is slowly changing as more and more women become cops, firefighters, top athletes, etc.). Director Brian De Palma told one interviewer, "Women in peril work better in the suspense genre. It all goes back to *The Perils of Pauline*. . . . If you have a haunted house and you have a woman walking around with a candelabrum, you fear for her more than you would for a husky man." De Palma insists that "female frailty" is "part of the suspense form."

While it may seem old-fashioned, it is a fact that for generations Americans have thought of men as "heroes" and women as "homemakers" who had to be protected by their men. Women could be plucky, spunky, and brave (or more often foolhardy), but in the end it was always Superman or some variation who came to the rescue of Lois Lane or one of her counterparts. This concept has been so ingrained in the public consciousness—it persists to this day in spite of

Female sacrifice (a popular storyline) in *Cry of the Banshee*.

the efforts of feminist movements—that it is no wonder both male and female writers and filmmakers employ the "woman in danger" device in suspense and horror films. Of course, there have been several films in which male protagonists are themselves over their heads and thoroughly victimized, such as *The Marathon Man* (1976), with Dustin Hoffman.

But in the late fifties the old woman-in-danger formula was given what some felt was a misogynistic twist in that the strings of female victims were killed not so much because of their frailty, nor because they couldn't fight off their attacker the way a husky six-foot football player could, but simply because they were female (as well as young and beautiful). It seemed filmmakers were recording simulated scenes of anti-female violence to exorcise their own feelings of insecurity and impotence with the opposite sex. Like Norman Bates, they were killing the pretty women they were unable to make love to. They were stabbing, skewering, mutilating, and scalding the beautiful, haughty "bitches" who teased them provocatively, but never delivered. The female victims in these movies were hardly ever ugly, old, or infirm—they were only the kinds of women who would attract and arouse the male viewer, and who then had to be killed for their sexual disdain or distance.

Gradually this formula became so commonplace that movies and books about maniacs and their female victims proliferated, in spite of the fact that some of the writers and directors were female, or men who had healthy, realistic attitudes toward women. To read sinister motives into all of these books and movies would be a gross error; just as the old *Perils of Pauline* serial gave birth to hundreds of imitations, so did these kill-the-pretty-girl pictures beget literally thousands of similar items. To take them as a collective attack upon womankind is to give them unfair notoriety; often these films had nothing more on their minds than getting some thrills and suspense across to the audience, usually by milking and retreading the same old tired formula without a single second of invention or variation.

The maniac in *The Burning* corners a female counselor (but he likes to kill the boys, too).

The infamous rape-strangulation scene from Hitchcock's *Frenzy*.

There are films that are undeniably mean-spirited and nasty in their attitude toward women. The problem is that many feminists and critics don't distinguish these films from those that may employ female victims, but do so without the lingering smarminess or vicious misogyny that makes the others so decidedly unpleasant. They also fail to understand that, often, movie violence—whether directed against men or women—is a vehicle for the director to show off his cinematic virtuosity, and usually not meant as a statement of his contempt.

Back in 1972 Alfred Hitchcock's *Frenzy* aroused the ire of feminists and others because of a fairly graphic rape/murder scene in the middle of the picture. The murderer places his victim on a couch and rips her dress to expose her breasts ("lovely, *lovely*," he intones). He then proceeds to sexually assault her while the poor, terrified woman shivers in fear and starts to murmur the Lord's Prayer. As the man's "ardor" increases, he unconsciously raises his voice, until he is practically shouting the word *lovely*. When he is finished sexually abusing the woman, he takes off his tie, wraps it around her neck, and strangles her.

Outraged social critics reacted to the scene as if Hitchcock had snarled "that'll teach the bitch" in every frame, and the males in the audience did the same. They also feared that the scene would inspire other men to go out and rape someone. But the scene isn't really arousing because Hitchcock concentrates as much on the woman as he does on the rapist. Her sobs, and her expression of terror make it clear that this is not an enjoyable or sensual moment. The audience is frightened for her. The scene is not a celebration of gratification. Hitchcock, the consummate professional, saw the rape/murder not as a turn-on but as a scene of action and suspense, which had to be considered, storyboarded, and then filmed with as much cinematic élan as any other scene. Hitchcock approached it not from the point of view of a pornographer, but from the level of pure filmmaking.

As for the charge that the scene might have inspired real-life rapes: The alarmingly high rape statistics suggest that men who engage in such practices don't have to go to the movies to get it into their minds.

Years later, Brian De Palma's films were coming under fire for similar reasons, and in the same way, De Palma has been misunderstood. His feminist critics forget that in his first *Psycho*-inspired thriller, *Sisters* (1973), it was a man who suffered a grisly butchershop death (at the hands of a psychotic female). There were no women victims in the film at all. Nevertheless, his later film, *Dressed to Kill* (1980), brought forth a storm of protest, particularly because of the scene wherein heroine Angie Dickinson is slashed to death with a straight razor in an elevator. Angered feminists charged that De Palma was a vicious woman-hater. At the beginning of the film Angie Dickinson has a rape fantasy while in the shower. Later that day she meets a strange man at a museum and returns to his apartment, where they have an adulterous encounter. She is slashed to death immediately thereafter. To the feminists the message was clear: Dickinson had to die because she had overstepped her bounds. She wanted to get raped, but got murdered instead.

Actually, Dickinson was killed off about forty minutes into the movie because Janet Leigh was killed off about forty minutes into *Psycho*, and *Dressed to Kill* was another of De Palma's homages to his favorite picture; nothing more, nothing less. De Palma was not trying to make harsh negative statements about women and sexuality. He was trying to mimic (or parody) a classic movie and entertain his audience at the same time. As for the infamous shower scene at the beginning of *Dressed to Kill*, it serves a dual purpose. First, Dickinson is not sexually satisfied by her husband's "slam-bam-thank-you-M'am" method of lovemaking, so she resorts to fantasizing. In that context she is not so much raped as taken by surprise. Second, *every* shower scene in a *Psycho* pastiche must be imbued with an element of suspense and ominousness; it's what the audience expects.

The controversial shower scene at the beginning of Brian De Palma's *Dressed to Kill*.

Whatever De Palma's motives for the female mayhem in *Dressed to Kill*, they exist in a decade when concerned citizens are far more sensitive (understandably so) to the issues of rape, misogyny, and violence against women. De Palma's admirers look at his films and see handsomely mounted suspense items that are impressive technical achievements. Feminists look at his films and simply see women being murdered.

Although feminists have objected to a number of films, never did they receive such widespread support as when a film entitled *Snuff* (distributed by Monarch Releasing Corp.) opened in 1976. The advertising slogan, MADE IN SOUTH AMERICA—*where life is cheap*, implied that the female victims in the film had actually been murdered. Eighty-two people in Manhattan, including feminists and many well-known artists, wrote to District Attorney Robert Morgenthau and asked him to close the picture. However, as John Leonard reported in *The New York Times*, the people from the protest committee who were delegated to sit through the movie discovered that the film was obviously a fake. However,

Leonard added, "The fact that the murder in *Snuff* is a counterfeit should have nothing to do with the fact that murder as sexual entertainment is pornographic." *Snuff* continued to play to packed houses.

Adding to all the controversy is the commonplace misconception that women are killed in slasher movies because they are independent or sexually promiscuous, daring to enjoy the sexual rights and privileges that have formerly been reserved for males. These movies are perceived as a backlash against women's liberation as well as a deadly double-standard message about the evils of immoral behavior. In both cases the interpretation is simplistic.

The victims in horror movies are often attacked during, immediately preceding, or immediately after the act of making love. This has been interpreted as proof that such films espouse conservative moral values. In other

A female victim about to get a whacking in *Pamela, Pamela You Are . . .*

PP-1

words, if you fool around, you die. Actually, the *raison d'etre* of such scenes is simply that they pander to the audience's delight in the sex-and-violence connection. Also, people making love are naked. Nude people, whether in the shower or in bed, are vulnerable. Nakedness also adds extra titillation. (Feminists object that it's usually female nudity that is used to titillate, but this criticism extends to all genres of film, not just horror.) While the films that have featured attacks on lovemaking couples are numerous, at least two films, *Twitch of the Death Nerve* (1971) and *Friday the 13th Part Two* (1981) have gone so far as to depict a couple being jointly impaled while in the midst of lovemaking.

The fact that the sexually active women in these films get murdered is simply an inevitable byproduct of the clichés and conventions of the genre. The notion that the makers of all these movies are old-fashioned moralists who are trying to get an anti-sex message across to their audience is ridiculous. Opponents of these films also blithely ignore the fact that many of these films have numerous male victims, as well as victims of either sex who are not killed while engaging in, or in the pursuit of, sexual pleasure, but rather in the midst of such mundane activities as washing laundry, making dinner, or watching the late show on TV.

Groups such as *Women Against Pornography* and *Women Against Violence Against Women* see women-as-victim films as just another pornographic expression of contempt for women. But even the worst of these pictures (as with the sleaziest sex magazines) are at best symptoms and not the cause of whatever misogynous attitudes may be inherent in our society. Wiping out sex magazines or women-in-danger films will do little to affect contemporary attitudes, especially when such comparatively innocent things as TV shows and humor magazines are just as sexist and chauvinistic as horror films and skin books.

There's no denying that women and other concerned parties have a right to protest these movies and to present their viewpoint, the same as other pressure groups (see Chapter Five). But underneath the clamor, there is the omnipresent specter of censorship. The fact remains that no one is ever forced to pay five bucks for the privilege of seeing a movie he finds oppressive.

A distinction must be made between films in which the plot revolves around a misogynous character who kills women (*He Knows You're Alone,* in which a man only murders brides-to-be), and those in which the filmmakers seem to revel in, even applaud, the maniac's grisly deeds. Of course, in either type of picture the filmmakers often show scenes of the killer doing his "thing" to women—killing them, debasing them, what have you. The latter films, however, present these deeds with a clinical, lipsmacking exactitude that can be considered pornographic. Low-grade thrillers such as *Don't Answer the Phone* (1980) consist almost entirely of vulgar scenes wherein the killer degrades and strangles young women. Many of these films also illustrate the link between sexism and

Critics charged that *Friday the 13th* was a sexist picture, but it's also a woman who's holding the knife.

homophobia by including gratuitous "fag" jokes in which stereotypical gay characters or drag queens are similarly debased, murdered, or at the very least, made fun of.

The script for *Phone* implies that the murderer (Nicholas Worth) kills women so that his dead, apparently macho, father will finally approve of him, but there is no attempt made to appeal to the cerebral instincts of the audience. A scriptwriter with talent and intelligence might have taken the basic formula and used it to say something about misogynous attitudes. For example, how they're passed from father to son, about the stress placed on men in society, the conflict between men and women in today's changing world. However, the emphasis of *Phone* is clearly and exclusively sick thrills for the women-haters in the audience.

Eyes of a Stranger (1981) is another lurid thriller, this time about a rapist/killer and the female reporter who tries to track him down. Although a couple of males are violently snuffed during the course of the film, the ambience of *Eyes* is as vulgar and sexist as *Phone's*. Ditto for *Schizoid* (1980), an uneven thriller about a lonelyhearts columnist who receives threatening letters while a maniac kills off the female members of her therapy group with a pair of scissors.

A similar thriller, *New Year's Evil* (1981), at least has a novel premise: a punk rock star (Roz Kelly) hosts a TV show celebrating New Year's Eve when a killer calls in to announce that he will murder a new victim at midnight in all four time zones of the United States. Not so novel is the killer's motive, the usual hatred of, in his eyes, conniving, manipulative women. *Visiting Hours* (1982) did make *some* attempt to comment on the problem of misogyny. In this one a prominent women's libber (that fine actress, Lee Grant), comes under attack from a woman-hating psycho who wounds her in his first assault, and murders about a half-dozen people trying to finish the job at the hospital where Grant is recovering. Though the film has its sleazier moments, and is as ineptly directed as all of the aforementioned "thrillers," it does have ample energy and is not as leeringly sexist as most of the others in the category.

The Eyes of Laura Mars (1978) is an interesting thriller that makes a stab at exploring the social issues involved in the violent (some feel misogynous) fashion photography of the seventies. Faye Dunaway plays a photographer obsessed with violent layouts. Her models pose in shots at the scene of fake automobile crashes, tear at each other's clothes, pull each other's hair, all to sell the latest trendy and expensive garments. Dunaway's friends and models become the victims of a particularly vicious killer who punctures their eyeballs with his weapon. Dunaway, a psychic, is able to see these murders as they progress (from the murderer's point of view). To make matters worse, the death scenes resemble many of the fashion layouts Dunaway has supervised. Except for one brief sequence when a female reporter tries to ask Dunaway if her photographs are offensive to women (she is quickly rebuffed), the movie never really deals with the issues it raises. Despite an excellent premise and some good sequences, the movie is devoid of sympathetic, well-developed characters and is all but ruined by Irvin Kershner's pedestrian direction.

It isn't just these formula women-in-danger pictures that have come under attack for misogynous attitudes. In his review of the supernatural "splatter film," *The Evil Dead*, in *Cinefantastique* Magazine, Joseph Francavilla writes: "But all could be forgiven (or at least forgotten) if it weren't for the creeping misogyny that finds its way into the empty storyline," which is about demons possessing

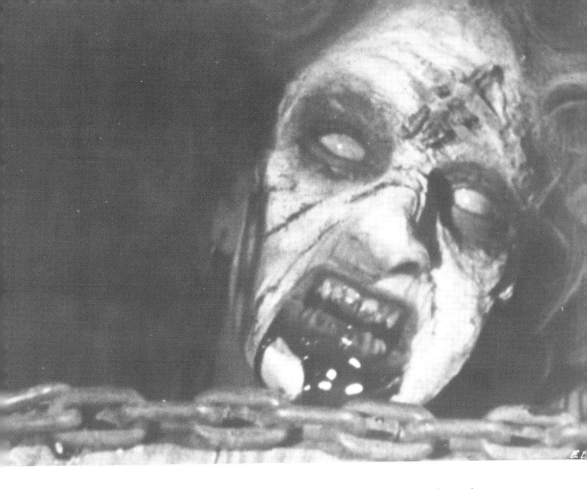

One of the possessed women who must be dismembered in *The Evil Dead*.

some of the five youths staying at an isolated cabin in the woods and causing them to attack the others. He continues, "The female characters are possessed by demons first, allowing the unpossessed male characters to maim and brutalize them. The women are hit, threatened by guns and chainsaws, pummeled with a large wooden beam, stabbed, chopped up into pieces with an axe and decapitated. Except for one brief scene of Scott's [Hal Delrich] possession, the women are the only ones who act 'demonic,' and hence 'deserve' to be trashed, hurt, tortured, etc."

Of course, it is debatable as to whether the makers of *The Evil Dead* deliberately intended to get such a message across, but what Francavilla says might suggest that on a subliminal level they made a film that could be taken by some as only an excuse to present scenes of anti-female abuse. It must be said, however, that the "possessed" parties of *The Evil Dead* are transformed into such demonic, slobbering horrors that it is hard to even think of them as being male or female, only animal.

In any case, the makers of sexist thrillers aren't disturbed in the least by the complaints of certain factions of the women's movement and other concerned individuals. None of the films already mentioned had an ad as blatant and sleazy as the one for *Girl's Nite* [sic] *Out* (1984), a campus slasher flick with Hal Holbrook. Interestingly enough, the film doesn't quite fall under the "women-as-victim" umbrella, but the publicity campaign does. The movie's ads showed a picture of a writhing, attractive, scantily clad woman tied to a wall, with the copy: *You know what really turned her on . . . she loved to be scared; weird and kinky things really got her motor running.* And in smaller print: *Don't bring your girlfriend to this film, she may never go out again.*

The anti-porn, anti-"mad slasher" segment of the women's movement is not supported by all women, or even by all feminists, for that matter. Author Rita Mae Brown wrote the screenplay for the violent *Slumber Party Massacre* (1983), which was directed by Amy Jones. The film, no different from a hundred other similar items written and directed by men, is about an escaped lunatic who terrorizes a group of high-school girls getting together for a night of fun and chatter. He kills them and their boyfriends with an electric drill, knives, and other destructive implements. A record amount of blood is shed on camera, and more than once director Jones films the action in such a way that an unavoidable corollary between drill and penis is made. (Brian De Palma came under fire for doing the same thing in *Body Double's* power drill murder scene.) Jones' camera ogles women's breasts and buttocks, and the movie comes off as far more leering and sexist than the pictures that are usually (and sometimes unfairly) cited as women-hater films (such as *Friday the 13th*), especially in that the misogynous killer in *Slumber Party* murders men only when they get in the way of the girls he's really after.

As distasteful as it all sounds, *Slumber Party* moves fast (once it gets going in the second half) and the bodies pile up so quickly (with a death, it seems, almost every five minutes) that the audience is carried along in the excessive ghoulishness to the point where it cheers the girls on when they finally turn the tables on their attacker and give him an all-too-fitting demise. The picture is similar to *Last House on the Left* (1972), which was also attacked by feminists. But both films seem critic-proof. They possess audience-participation energy; filmgoers thrill and chill to the action, despite their urge to recoil from the considerable bloodletting.

In the final analysis, however, *Slumber Party* betrays its slapdash weaknesses on a second viewing, when there's no hollering audience to add excitement to the proceedings. (In fact, most of these stalk-and-slash films don't cut it more than once.) Whatever its faults, though, *Slumber Party* is at least better (and less misogynous) than total garbage like *Don't Answer the Phone*. Nevertheless, feminists were outraged by the picture and felt betrayed. In a televised interview, Jones said she felt they were taking the movie and its violence much too seriously.

Clearly, women who make violent films of horror aren't going to be let off easily by their feminist counterparts. The *Variety* review of *Streetwalkin'* (1985), which, like *Vice Squad* (1982), is a crime melodrama with horror movie elements, including the obligatory psycho, said: "[Director] Joan Freeman apparently favors scenes in which characters, usually young women, are brutally and continually beaten. Then there are the shootings and stabbings—lots of them. . . . Despite the presence of a femme director at the helm, feminists will undoubtedly be outraged."

After an article about the making of the 3D slasher film, *Silent Madness*, appeared in *The New York Times* magazine section,[9] a letter by a female reader had this to say: "Forget about the writer, director, producer and distributor. The real perpetrators of this pornography are the actresses who agreed to perform, or who even *considered* performing, in this film."

Slumber Party Massacre's final scene of female vengeance brings to mind other controversial pictures in which women are at first captured and demeaned, but then manage to get even with the male slobs who have abused them. Perhaps the most infamous is *I Spit On Your Grave*, which is cited by the feminists and others as a prime example of women-hating sleaze (because of the first section, in which a woman is abused by a party of men), but which details (in the second half) the same woman's brutal vengeance upon her attackers.

Mother's Day (1980) has a similar theme: A wacky mother (the excellent Rose Ross) and two demented sons who live in a messy house in the backwoods capture three vacationing women, torment, rape, and ultimately murder one of them, only to face the bloody, terrible vengeance of the two surviving women. Director/writer Charles Kaufman tries for something different, with a lot of bizarre, clever touches, and more characterization than one is accustomed to in these films. The young women—three close friends who used to be college roommates—give excellent performances, and their relationships are delineated just enough to make you care about and root for them. The humiliation scenes are strong and tasteless, forgivable only because of the brutal finale, when the women get even. They chop one guy in the groin with a hatchet, slice another up with an electric kitchen knife, and suffocate the wicked mother without mercy.

What the critics of movies like *Mother's Day* don't seem to understand is that revenge dramas *do not work* unless the filmmakers give sufficient cause for the audience to emotionally identify with the ones who are getting revenge. Not showing in graphic form the debasement of the victims (regardless of sex) deprives the climactic paybacks of all power and purpose.

The female victim fights back against her attacker in *Friday the 13th Part Two*.

Social critics make much of the fact that male audience members cheer on the misogynous misfits in these movies as they rape, plunder, and murder their screaming, writhing female victims. Since these same critics walk out of the moviehouse in disgust long before the movie is over, they don't realize that these same men cheer on (with renewed enthusiasm, in fact) the heroines, who are often as strong, sexy, and independent as the victims, as they blow away the killer with a shotgun or get him between the eyes with a machete. All of these men are said to be identifying with the maniac, but they enjoy *his* death throes the most of all, and applaud the heroine with admiration.

The vast majority of contemporary shockers, whether in the sexist mold or not, feature climaxes in which women fight back against their attackers—the wandering, humorless psychos who populate these films. They often show more courage and levelheadedness than their cringing male counterparts. Scenes in which women whimper helplessly and do nothing to defend themselves (such as

Yvonne Mitchell (left) and Sharon Gurney team up to get rid of their male oppressor in *Crucible of Horror*.

a particularly idiotic scene in *Don't Open Till Christmas*, 1984) are ridiculed by the audience, who find it hard to believe that anyone—male or female—would simply allow someone to kill them with nary a protest.

There have been occasional films in which the psychotic murderers are themselves women, such as several of the "aging-actress" horror films of the sixties (see Chapter Eight). *Hands of the Ripper, The Creeping Flesh, Play Misty for Me, Deep Red,* and *Sisters* are several notable thrillers of the seventies that feature homicidal females. The trend resurfaced in the late seventies and eighties, with female maniacs in *Friday the 13th* (first installment only), *Night School, Silent Scream,* and others. No doubt using women as the psychos instead of the victims isn't particularly endearing to the feminists, either. Besides, most of the *victims* in these films are also female. The engrossing, vivid *Crucible of Horror* (1971), however, is about a more-or-less normal mother and daughter who team up to kill off the tyranical head of the household, sort of a "burning bed" type of self-defense. Films in which women murder only male victims are few and far between, with *Ms. 45* (1981) one of the better-known items.

The use of women as victims in horror films is not likely to change in the near future. Director Dario Argento, interviewed in *Cinefantastique* by Alan Jones (September 1983), had this to say on the subject: "I like women, especially beautiful ones. If they have a good face and figure, I would much prefer to watch them being murdered than an ugly girl or a man."

TERROR AND CONTROVERSY

Horror films, particularly multiple-murder shockers, have come under attack from various segments of society for any number of reasons. The previous chapter detailed the feminist argument against movies in which strings of helpless female victims are carved up and often sexually assaulted. This chapter focuses on the psychiatric community's reaction to *The Twisted Nerve*, the heavily publicized flap the gay community caused over *Cruising*, the housewives' brouhaha over *Silent Night, Deadly Night*, and the "stalk-and-slash" movie controversy.

The Twisted Nerve engendered some minor controversy when it was released in 1969. A British chiller directed by Roy Boulting, it stars Hywel Bennet as twenty-one-year-old "Georgie Clifford," a young man who leaves his home and unpleasant parents and goes to a London boarding house, where he is befriended by the landlady (Billie Whitelaw) and her librarian-daughter (Hayley Mills). Before long, Whitelaw is making passes at Bennett, and he's going off on a homicidal rampage. Howard Thompson of *The New York Times* found the film "more unsettling than rewarding, and certainly more contrived than compassionate," and reported that "the strangest thing about it—and the point of the picture—is the homestretch disclosure hereditarily linking [Georgie's] explosive carnage, and a twisted chromosome, to the existence of a mongoloid brother."

It was this disclosure that so upset some members of the psychiatric establishment that the picture carried a disclaimer requested by the National Association for Retarded Children. It stated that "there is no established scientific connection between Mongolism and psychotic or criminal behavior."

Archer Winsten of the *New York Post* was not impressed with NARC's objections. "Actually, the picture puts the two (Mongolism and the behavior of the psychopath) together only in the sense that they're brothers and that they both got their mental make up by means of parental chromosomes." Ann

Billie Whitelaw (right) hasn't learned the first law of horror movies: Never make a pass at a psychopath (Hywel Bennett in *The Twisted Nerve*).

Guarino of the *New York Daily News*, however, found *Twisted Nerve* to be "creepy and sick."

Andrew Sarris of the *Village Voice* had the last laugh: "For a project directed and produced by her husband, Roy Boulting, it is a curious thing to have more references in the dialogue to Hywel Bennett's good looks than to Hayley Mills'."

For whatever reasons, *Twisted Nerve* seems to have disappeared from the face of the earth, rarely, if ever, showing up on television or in revival theaters.

Perhaps the shocker that brought about the biggest outcry from a special interest group was William Friedkin's *Cruising* (1980). The film is based on a novel by Gerald Walker in which an undercover cop is assigned to investigate a series of gruesome murders in the homosexual community. The officer is troubled by his own homosexual feelings, and it is implied at the end that after his first gay experience he will take up where the actual killer has left off.

The book was controversial because, in spite of a moderately sympathetic viewpoint, it presents a homosexual world that is bleak, distasteful, neurotic, and miserable, in vivid contrast to the new attitudes brought about by the efforts of gay liberationists. In Walker's novel homosexuality and pathology seem inseparably intermingled, as though, with certainty, gay sex leads to death. It's no wonder that when news of a planned movie version got out, the gay community was more than a little disturbed.

The irony of the situation was that the director of *Cruising*, William Friedkin, also directed the film version of Mart Crowley's play, *The Boys in the Band* (1970), a no-holds-barred look at a homosexual birthday party in which a diverse group of gay men castigate and psychologically expose themselves and each other. Unfortunately, some members of the gay community considered *Boys* (both play and movie) to have been terribly dated even at the time of the film's release—just another fictional treatment of gays that inspired pity perhaps (and, inevitably, contempt), but not equality. The book, *Cruising*, plus the director, Friedkin, made for a volatile combination.

Hayley Mills sees something awful in *The Twisted Nerve*. The reviews?

Al Pacino (right) discusses gay life with a friend in *Cruising*.

Word about the movie shot through the community, alerting various gay rights activists, among the most prominent of whom was the late Arthur Bell, columnist and reporter for the weekly *Village Voice*. Bell used his column to ring an alarm throughout New York's rather large homosexual community, and at a press conference accused Friedkin of being a bigot.

Generally, the gay community was not in favor of completely censoring the film, but it *was* outraged to learn that Friedkin planned to do location filming right in the bars and streets of the famous "gay ghetto" in Greenwich Village. That, they felt, was adding insult to injury. "If you must make the movie, make it in the studio in Hollywood," Friedkin was told, more or less. "Don't exploit us further by using actual gay bars and homosexual actors."

Friedkin was not deterred. He was getting tons of free publicity, for one thing. And so, for that matter, was the gay community. Newspapers and magazines were finally paying attention to their outcries. Everyone seemed satisfied . . . until the filming began.

Every time Friedkin set up his crew outside a bar or along a Greenwich Village street, gay protestors gathered en masse on the site to boo, chant, and distract the performers. They put up such a clamor that it was said Friedkin would have to employ extensive studio dubbing to recapture lost lines of dialogue and stifle the background noises of the crowd.

Although Walker's novel ignored the sado-masochistic, or leather, subculture of the gay community, Friedkin wisely understood that the basic pulp horror story would make more sense if juxtaposed against an S-and-M backdrop. Out-of-work leathermen in their caps and tight black jeans were called on duty to play themselves in gay bar sequences (with extra money going to those who would enact simulated sex scenes). Fueled by reports in the papers, a minor civil war broke out in the gay community. Protestors accused the gay extras of being self-oppressive traitors, and the leathermen-turned-actors accused the protestors of trying to discriminate against the subculture to which they belonged. Undoubtedly there were gay activists who felt the leathermen were not a fit image to represent the gay community, for, like effeminate drag queens, they are only one segment of it. However, most protestors objected not to the depiction of gay sado-masochism in *Cruising* but to the way the movie reduced gay characters to one-dimensional victims. Actually, some of the film's most vocal protestors were themselves leathermen.

More and more stories about the controversy appeared in New York's local papers, and eventually the protest got national coverage. Arthur Bell got into feuds with other columnists, most notably the liberal Pete Hamill (then of the *New York Daily News*), who was sympathetic to gays, but felt their protests were oppressive and fascistic, and with Rex Reed (also then of the *News*) who complained acidly that Bell's stories about grisly gay murders in the *Voice* were far more homophobic than anything in Friedkin's movie. Not to be outdone, the vituperative Bell retaliated months later by writing an article for the *Voice* in which he alleged that much of Reed's work was ghost-written.

Meanwhile, some gays felt that the protests over the film were only giving the movie undue attention and would serve to increase its box-office receipts when it finally opened. Protestors countered that Friedkin had become such an "important" director after the success of *The Exorcist* (see Chapter Six) that *Cruising* would receive much press coverage regardless of public reaction.

For weeks on end, there was stormy debate over the issue. *Cruising's* proponents argued that the gay community was making too much over the sexual orientation of the characters in the film, that Friedkin was simply adapting an interesting, unusual, and highly erotic thriller and not trying to discriminate against or exploit anyone in particular. Opponents argued that it was hardly fair to make a movie that employed a gay backdrop only for the purpose of sleazy thrills, without at the same time trying to educate the public about the subject, particularly when, unlike heterosexuals, several million gay Americans were still being deprived of their civil rights.

Al Pacino (left) and Richard Cox have a park encounter in *Cruising*.

It was also hard not to notice that *Cruising* was really just the same old "kill the pretty girls" story, substituting male homosexuals for beautiful women. (Not a happy comparison for those masculine gay men who, unlike "queens," identify with the male sex.) It's the old double standard: heterosexual men can have sex to their heart's content and people will call them studs. Women do the same thing and they're derided as whores. Sexually active gay men are labeled sick. Applying this double standard to horror movies, women and gays become deserving victims. Films in which strings of straight men are hacked at or sexually assaulted are few and far between.

The protest continued, and eventually Friedkin packed up his cameras, cast, and crew and flew back to Hollywood. Apparently he decided that many of the scenes he had planned to film in Greenwich Village would work just as well in the studio.

The controversy died down while the movie was being finished, edited, and readied for distribution. But only a few weeks before it opened in theaters in 1980, along came another little item that almost escaped the notice of the gay community and everyone else.

The film was called *Windows*, and it was a total mistake from conception to execution. Apparently, all the uproar over *Cruising* didn't have an impact on United Artists, which was releasing both films. *Windows* is about a psychotic lesbian (Elizabeth Ashley, a fine actress who needs a better agent), who preys upon the woman who is the object of her dreams (mousey Talia Shire). A handsome police officer (Joe Cortese) comes between them. Incredibly United Artists brought this out in early 1980, shortly before the release of *Cruising*.

Windows had been filmed in such secrecy that it snuck up on everyone, the gay community and the general public alike, with little if any fanfare. It was the directorial debut of Gordon Willis, the enormously gifted cinematographer of such films as *The Godfather, All the President's Men, Manhattan*, and *Klute*. To say it did for gay women what *Cruising* did for gay men is an understatement.

As to be expected, Willis' expert cinematography is the picture's only saving grace. *Windows* was sumptuously photographed almost entirely on New York City locations, primarily Brooklyn Heights. One screening of the film was attended by a goodly number of young women from the group Lesbian Feminist Liberation (LFL). The comments from that audience were far more entertaining than the picture, which, as one person put it, was "the worst film of 1980—and it's only February!"

The members of LFL were particularly perturbed by a scene in which Talia Shire is raped, especially because it turns out that the assailant was hired by Elizabeth Ashley in the hope that the brutal incident would forever turn love-object Shire away from men. "It's men who hurt women," one woman shouted at the screen. "Not other women!"

True, it is utterly ridiculous to suggest that any woman, any person, in fact, would want to have someone she loved raped, beaten, and humiliated, for any purpose whatsoever. Although the people associated with *Windows* argued that Ms. Ashley was playing a psychotic who "happened to be" a lesbian, and not a "typical" gay woman, critics agreed that in these days of discrimination and misunderstanding, the picture's plot was tasteless and irresponsible.

Even as a thriller, *Windows* is utterly useless. The picture seems to consist entirely of handsomely lighted but hilarious shots of a very intense Liz Ashley peering at the listless, moping Shire through a telescope she has trained on the building across the way. (What she sees in her is never apparent.) Clearly the audience is supposed to be repulsed by the attention one woman is paying another, no matter how much the film's creators have said otherwise. During the rest of the picture nutty Ashley murders two men (offscreen), and for some reason puts Shire's poor little kitty in the freezer! The finale, in which stalwart Cortese rescues Shire from the clutches of lesbian Ashley, generates absolutely no thrills or tension. The film laid a bomb as big as Texas, and was quickly, almost immediately, forgotten by stay-away audiences and everyone else.

The production notes on *Windows* read: "Because of the highly unusual"—i.e. gay—"nature of the storyline, *Windows* was filmed on closed sets, and the cast and production crew were pledged to secrecy when it came to discussing the movie." It would have been better for all concerned, including screenwriter Barry Siegel, if United Artists had chosen to keep *Windows* a secret from the audience.

Not long after *Windows* disappeared without a trace, *Cruising*, the film for which it had been a mere warmup, finally opened. The gay community wasted no time in getting out placards and picketing theaters that showed the movie. Pamphlets and flyers detailing exactly why *Cruising* was oppressive were dstributed. News reports focused on public reaction.

Regardless of whether *Cruising* is an oppressive film, the fact remains that it's a pretty lousy one. Reportedly, Friedkin did manage to capture the ambience of certain gay leather bars, and the film is consistently atmospheric, but the murder scenes are not entirely successful, and the whole production—from cinematography down to musical score—is only fair to middling. The continuity and storyline are so choppy that the identity of the killer preying on homosexual men is never ascertained. The physical build of the major suspect is not the same as that of the man we see committing the murders earlier in the picture.

There is a lot of sexual energy in the film, but *Cruising*'s portrayal of the gay community is on a cartoon level, filled with precious dialogue and flippant confrontations that garner more laughs than chills. In a park encounter between two cruising men, one fellow says to the other, "hips or lips?" his caricatured way of asking whether they should engage in fellatio or sodomy. At another point two gays are dressed half in leather and half in drag, a combination that—according to gay reviewers—would hardly occur in real life as drag queens and leathermen operate under entirely different compulsions. Apparently, filming in the streets of Greenwich Village did not necessarily result in a great deal of accuracy.

As the protestors feared, the gay characters in the movie are made of cardboard, and the movie makes no attempt to seriously probe the realities or positive qualities of the homosexual lifestyle. Supposedly, in an effort to placate his detractors, Friedkin toned down his original ending so that it is no longer quite clear if the undercover cop, as in the novel, has already or will become a murderer himself. However, certain muddled implications are made, such as, exposure to the gay S-and-M community is corrupting and insidious. That this exposure leads to pathological homicidal tendencies is a dubious hypothesis at best and an irresponsible insinuation at worst.

It is unlikely that Friedkin was even interested in delving into the mysteries of gay life or of anti-gay prejudice. His follow-ups to *The Exorcist*—a shocking film that had broken a lot of rules—had not been very successful. He felt that by tackling the subject matter of *Cruising* he would once again be considered "daring," or, more to the point, newsworthy. It was a ploy that didn't work.

Cruising was neither a critical nor a financial success. Whether reviewers disliked the film because of its anti-gay exploitative aspects or simply because they found its homosexual overtones distasteful was not always clear, but the picture was thoroughly trounced by most of them. Friedkin, once a promising director, is no longer in the limelight, and the movie also did nothing for the career of Al Pacino, who plays the cop-protagonist. His little touches—such as when he puts on eye makeup before going out to a leather bar (supposedly places where stereotypical effeminacy is disdained)—do nothing to sharpen his characterization or add to the movie's veracity.

After all that fuss and bother, *Cruising* disappeared from theaters almost as fast as *Windows* did. The failure of the two pictures has probably contributed to the dearth of subsequent movies dealing with gay subject matter, though thrillers

Christopher Reeve (left) wrestles with Michael Caine in *Deathtrap*.

with gay undertones (usually negative) show up on occasion. *Best Friends* (not to be confused with the Goldie Hawn/Burt Reynolds comedy) is billed as a melodrama in which repressed homosexuality causes trouble for the characters, but the film is rarely seen outside of cable. *Deathtrap* (1982) received wide exposure mostly because it co-starred *Superman's* Christopher Reeve, not because it was based on Ira Levin's hit Broadway play. This tale of two typically amoral bisexuals (an older playwright and a budding competitor) who love no one but themselves is another example of a vehicle that uses homosexuality for titillation and added repugnance without bothering to seriously examine or illuminate the subject.

One homosexually oriented suspense film that should be mentioned, however, is *The Fourth Man*, a 1984 import from Holland. The homosexual aspects of the plot are handled quite matter–of–factly, not in the usual self-conscious Hollywood manner. The hero, a gruff, burly bisexual with a preference for men, though hardly a likable person, is neither fey nor tormented. He might be characterized, though, as just another in a long line of immoral and irresponsible fictional bi's. That plus the fact that his lover (seen only at the beginning of the film) is a "bitchy young queen" indicates that *The Fourth Man* is not really attempting to approach the subject matter in a more radical manner than its precursors. The film, however, does not try to link homosexuality and psychopathology, exploit the gay community or make a big to-do out of the protagonist's sex life.

What distinguishes *The Fourth Man* is its style and story line. Director Paul Verhoeven has mastered the Hitchcockian device of investing humorous scenes with menace, and the movie is full of portents, premonitions, and forewarnings. Often it is at its creepiest when it is most humorous, but it would be wrong to label this brooding, absorbing picture a comedy.

The story has to do with a writer who becomes the lover of a beautiful young woman (well played by the striking Renee Soutendijk) solely for the purpose of getting closer to her handsome young boyfriend. But as he experiences intimacy with both, the writer finds out that the woman has been married three times—and that each of her previous husbands died under mysterious circumstances. Is she a murderess? And who will be her fourth husband—or fourth *victim*—the *fourth man* of the title, the writer or the handsome young man who indirectly got him involved with the lady in the first place?

The Fourth Man is not a typical thriller in either style or plot, but it's very well-acted and beautifully crafted. It carries its share of shocks, too, including a climactic, gory auto crash where one of the above-mentioned men gets a steel pole thrust through his eye. The problem with the picture is that the director is so busy detailing the (often religious) symbolism and crafting bizarre (often sexual) imagery—such as when the hero imagines his handsome young prey in

Jeroen Krabbé (right) is convinced that lovely Renée Soutendijk is a murderess in *The Fourth Man*.

the place of a lifesize crucifix—that he never really bothers to clear up the picture's questions and provide a solid answer to the murder mystery itself. The movie just sort of fades away at the end, as if it were an "art picture" above such petty things as logic and plausibility. In spite of that it remains a worthwhile attempt and one of the few recent movies that can legitimately be labelled "Hitchcockian."

Silent Night, Deadly Night would be an absolutely unremarkable movie were it not for the controversy that surrounded its opening in November 1984. It is unlikely that any of the people protesting the picture actually bothered to go see it, because the protests were caused not by the movie itself, but by its television advertisements, particularly one shot of a maniacal Santa Claus wielding an axe. "He knows when you've been naughty," intoned the advertising slogan.

Just as *Cruising* elicited protests from the liberal camp, *Silent Night*'s opponents were of a more conservative bent. Parents, particularly Denise Giordano of the Bronx, N.Y., were outraged at the thought of a film that would make Santa Claus a villain, and a murderous one at that. "I have a very impressionable three-year-old child," Giordano told one interviewer. Apparently it did not matter to the protestors that the villain in the picture only dressed as Santa Claus (he was not supposed to actually be the mythical figure), or that three-year-olds, impressionable or otherwise, were hardly the target audience for this gory, R-rated horror film, which was no different than a dozen other stalk-and-slash films.

Nonetheless, the film's producer, Ira Barmak, agreed that the advertisements for the picture should have been shown on television only late at night. Perhaps if that had happened, there would have been no protests. Ms. Giordano and her ilk managed to give the picture a great deal of free publicity. A Bronx moviehouse was picketed. One placard read: DECK THE HALLS WITH HOLLY, NOT BODIES. People in other cities where the picture was showing registered protests with moviehouses, PTAs, and groups such as *Action for Children's TV*. New York State Assemblyman Neil Kelleher (R, Troy) started a campaign to boycott theaters showing the picture. For a while these pro-censorship advocates, whatever their motives, apparently forgot what country they were in, interfering with other people's, adults', right to see the picture. Unlike the *Cruising* protestors, they were not afraid *Silent Night* might contribute to the continued curtailment of anyone's civil liberties, but rather were simply promoting a personal definition of morality.

It all seemed like a pointless brouhaha once the advertisement was moved from the prime-time slot. Impressionable children who still believed in Santa Claus were hardly likely to go see *Silent Night*, which was geared, as Barmak put it, to "teenagers over 17 and young adults who go to these pictures like they go on roller coasters." Besides, reviews, or the newspaper ad itself, made it clear to prospective viewers that *Silent Night* was no *E.T.*

Several theaters dropped the picture before its standard two-week run was up, and its distributor, Tri-Star Pictures, canceled plans to show the picture on the West Coast. (It had been playing in 400 theaters in the northeast and midwest only.) The housewives' campaign seems to have been effective. Although *Silent Night* made back its low one-million-dollar production cost in the first week, business dropped off after the TV adds were discontinued (it might have done so in any case). With movie producers and production companies, protests generally fall on deaf ears. Money is all that matters.

What is especially interesting about the controversy is that *Silent Night* was not the first motion picture to feature a "killer Santa Claus." Two similar films had been made in 1980. *Variety* reported that *You Better Watch Out* (a.k.a. *Christmas Evil*), a production from the prolific Ed Pressman, also featured a maniac dressed in a Santa Claus suit. It played on 42nd Street during Christmas week in 1983, without TV or newspaper advertisements. *To All a Goodnight*, produced by Jay Rasumny, concerns a nut in a Santa Claus outfit who kills young women and their boyfriends at the Calvin Finishing School for Girls. It has not been released theatrically, but can be seen on videocassette. Also, the horror anthology film, *Tales from the Crypt* (1972), features a story in which Joan Collins is menaced by a crazed Kris Kringle.

To further confuse the issue, a picture entitled *Don't Open Till Christmas* (1984), an English import, opened in New York about two or three weeks after *Silent Night* did. In this one the idea is reversed: instead of a maniac Santa Claus, there's a maniac going around killing anyone who's *dressed* as Santa Claus. Although quite badly directed by its star, Edmund Purdom, the film is more involved and interesting than the usual mad-slasher flick, and features a few suspenseful and clever moments.

The same can be said for *Silent Night, Deadly Night*, whose intriguing, if terribly derivative, script by Michael Hickey is pretty much undermined by Charles E. Sellier, Jr.'s uninspired direction. The film's young star, Robert Brian Wilson, who plays the murderer, claims that the script was tampered with. "They pushed the story out the door and replaced it with gore," he told interviewer Kristin McMurray in *People*. Traces of an interesting plotline, opportunities for

The evil Mother Superior exerts an unhealthy influence over her troubled young charge in *Silent Night, Deadly Night*.

saying things and dealing with serious issues thus go unresolved and unrealized.

A little boy, Billy, is frightened when he and his parents visit his grandfather at the institution where the old man is being cared for. Although the grandfather is mute around everyone else, when he is alone with the boy he gives him a creepy message about "watching out" for Santa Claus. The boy is further traumatized on the drive home, when a man dressed in a Santa Claus suit—who has just robbed a store and shot the proprietor—commandeers their car and kills his parents.

A short while later, at the orphanage to which he has been sent, Billy is subjected to the evil ministrations of the Mother Superior, a nasty "wicked nun" stereotype who knows of Billy's Christmastime trauma but refuses to give him any concessions because of it. Another, kinder nun tries to protect Billy, but he still winds up tied to the bed by the Mother Superior as punishment for his alleged transgressions.

Years later he is a handsome young man who is strong enough to get a job as a stockclerk at a store during the holiday season rush. The Mother Superior's influence has given him an old-fashioned, lopsided view of morality. He is shy and sexually repressed. Furthermore, his discomfort over the time of the year and what it represents to him makes him seem a little weird—albeit likable—to the people he works with.

It all comes to a head Christmas Eve. The man who usually dresses up as Santa for the customers' children is sick. Will Billy take over? As soon as he gets into the uniform, he begins to change. Finally, during a small after-hours Christmas party, the rage and psychosis inside Billy come to a boil. Finding a co-worker forcing his advances on a pretty clerk in the storeroom, he passes sentence on the "sinner" and strangles him. He then dispatches the horrified girl with a knife.

After finishing off the others in the store, he goes on a rampage through the town while on his way out to the orphanage to settle accounts with the Mother Superior. Billy breaks into the orphanage, and is just about to kill the old woman when the police shoot him down from behind. It is implied that one or more of the children who witness this may themselves become unhinged due to the trauma of watching Santa Claus drop dead before their eyes.

Undoubtedly there is much in this film to disturb those who protested it—brief softcore sex scenes, the Mother Superior's hateful portrayal—and their outcries would probably have intensified had they actually sat through it. For those of a more open mind, however, the film is harmless and pedestrian, although it must be said that the scene in the prologue, when the killer exposes Billy's mother's breasts before stabbing her, is gratuitous and sleazy. But then, good taste has not always been this genre's strong point.

The whole Santa Claus controversy is reminiscent of the furor over horror

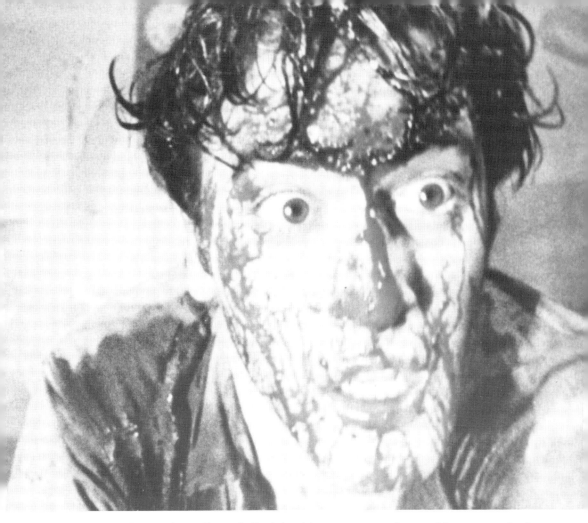

A "splatter" scene from *The Evil Dead*. Social critics oppose such graphic portrayal of violence.

comic books in the fifties. EC comic books like *Tales from the Crypt* and *Vault of Horror* (later turned into successful anthology films) and their many competitors were all the rage thirty years ago. But some people got it into their heads that these undeniably gruesome comics were responsible for an increase in juvenile delinquency. They argued that most of the youthful hoodlums in jails and reform schools were great fans of horror comic books, (yet so were millions of decent youngsters).

A psychologist, Dr. Frederic Wertham, wrote a book attacking the comics industry and its preoccupation with bloodshed entitled *Seduction of the Innocent*, which helped bring about the end of the horror comic books and forced the industry to establish a self-regulating comics code. The EC Horror Comics, and several other companies, had to fold.

IN DEFENSE OF HORROR

The audience sits in a darkened theater watching someone being stalked by a vicious psycho. First, someone gets a hatchet in the face. Then a shotgun blasts off someone else's head. A young woman is pursued by a psychopath who terrorizes, abuses, humiliates, and murders her. Victims of both sexes are garroted, stabbed, and dismembered. For whatever reasons, this sort of thing constitutes entertainment for millions of people.

Originally, horror films concentrated on vampires, werewolves, and Franken-stein's monster. These were horrors no one could really believe in. They were the stuff of nightmares, the ghosts and goblins that went bump in the dark. But the trend toward realism began in earnest with *Psycho*. The exploits of seemingly nice, normal men and women who happened to have an axe up their sleeve became the plots, depicted in gory detail, of mainstream horror films. This shift seemed to say, "This could happen to you."

Daily, sensational newspapers' headlines advertise vicious murders perpe-trated by antisocial misfits, and these situations have been mirrored, with incremental frequency, in horror films since the 1960s. Rape and dismember-ment are reported in newspapers with disheartening persistence. Fictionalized versions of these atrocities wind up in films like *Pieces* (1984) and *Eyes of a Stranger* (1981). Son of Sam, the Hollywood Strangler, and the Subway Slasher were real people with real victims. Movies have focused on their fictional counterparts such as *Madman* Marx and Jason Vorhees of the *Friday the 13th* series. Disturbed people develop obsessions for glamorous celebrities whom they follow about, threaten, and in whose names they sometimes murder. *The Fan* (1981) and *The Seduction* (1982) presented Lauren Bacall and Morgan Fairchild, respectively, as the unwilling objects of a psychotic's unwanted attentions.

Along with an insistence on realism (of a kind) in story lines, horror films exhibit their acts of murder and mayhem in a far more explicit manner than

Death is never cleaned up in today's gory shockers. (*Friday the 13th.*)

before. This trend began with *Psycho's* flamboyant shower murder. Although Hitchcock's classic sequence shows very little blood, it did put more emphasis on the murder itself than on the solving of it. Hitchcock continued in this groundbreaking tradition with a famous sequence in his spy thriller *Torn Curtain* (1966), wherein Paul Newman and a farm woman desperately try to kill off a police agent who is about to expose them. First they try to stab him with a knife that breaks. They then unsuccessfully attempt to strangle him. Finally, they are forced to knock him to his knees with a shovel and drag him over to an oven, where they make him inhale gas until he dies. It is one of the finest murder sequences in film, in that it goes beyond its thrills and considerable technical virtuosity to show the difficulty in taking a human life and the *enormity* of the action.

Today's splatter movies have taken this a step further (though less artfully, unfortunately), in that death is portrayed in all its ugliness. Each gash and wound is subjected to close-up examination, every drop of blood realistically gushing in splashing crimson glory. Many people credit Herschell Gordon Lewis' grade-Z drive-in "classic" *Blood Feast* (1963) with being the first out and out "gore film," but the movie was too poorly made and too outrageously awful to have had much impact. In the late sixties, films in general became more graphic, in depiction both of sex and violence, a result of the relaxation of censorship standards and both audiences' and filmmakers' insistence on a more honest approach. Even westerns and gangster films, like *The Wild Bunch* (1969) and *Bonnie and Clyde* (1967), were featuring shot-out eyes and blood-spattered, bullet-riddled bodies. Horror films, which by their very nature concentrate on the truly awful things that happen to people, inevitably had to go to extremes to reflect this trend.

Another reason for the explicitness of contemporary horror films is the cinema's technological sophistication. There has long been a theory that the best horror is unseen, that filmmakers can't possibly come up with anything as terrifying as the audience's imagination can. Certainly that was the case for many of the schlocky monster movies made in the forties and fifties, but today's makeup artists and special-effects men are capable of so many outstanding feats of terror and cinema magic that filmmakers often outdo the audience's imagination. Old-time monsters and makeup often looked ridiculous—with such exceptions as Lon Chaney's brilliant creations, and the effects in *Bride of Frankenstein* (1935), *King Kong* (1933), and a few other classics. Modern-day monsters and makeup sometimes look uncomfortably like the real thing—and worse. There's no doubt that too many contemporary directors rely on unimaginative splatter to get their point across. Others simply decide to show more in order to take advantage of the remarkable technological and makeup advances in the motion picture field.

To prevent people from being completely repulsed by the explicit nature of the onscreen activities, some shockers have built-in safeguards that distance the audience from the gore and the pain. These films add an element of unreality to the grim proceedings. In some cases the film has a supernatural slant, or the maniac is a monstrous, inhuman creature or alien horror that no one could possibly run into. *Halloween's* mad slasher, Michael Myers, qualifies as a monster, for instance, because he is impervious to mortal injury. Other films caricature the violence or exaggerate it to such an extent that it reaches comic book extremes. The ferocious, vicious nature of the action in *The Evil Dead* is almost like that of a particularly macabre cartoon. Sometimes it is the situations themselves that are overblown and fantastical. For instance, mass murders and massacres, such as the Manson cult slayings, are not uncommon, but the popular story of the summer-camp slaughter movie, *Friday the 13th* (a bereaved middle-aged mother kills off counselors because of the death of her son years ago), is so far-fetched that it becomes amusing.

In shockers that take place in a more realistic milieu and that depict the more or less unexaggerated exploits of "ordinary" killers, such as *Nightmare* (1981) and *Maniac* (1981), the distancing effect is provided by the shadowy characterizations of the victims. They are one-dimensional figures who are introduced into the plot only so that they can be murdered for the thrill of the audience. Their deaths are not particularly disturbing because the audience has not come to know them as people.

The gruesome murders in contemporary shockers are often quite hard to look at because they are extreme in their brutality and bloodiness. However, they don't whitewash death or make it seem prettier than it is. Even the films of directors such as Dario Argento and Brian De Palma, which are so elegantly choreographed and sumptously lighted that they almost make murder seem sensual, are pretty raw. In contrast, old movie westerns repeatedly showed· people being shot and punctured with arrows, but there was rarely any blood or gruesome wounds. Cowboys and Indians alike simply tumbled from their horses and expired with a sigh. Certain biological facts with regard to dead or injured bodies were ignored, such as the way arterial blood can spurt. (People who die violently also tend to lose control of their bodily functions. Fortunately contemporary horror films rarely dwell on that!) Death seemed like the easiest, most sanitary and frivolous thing in the world.

In multiple-murder films that are not shockers, such as the adaptations of Agatha Christie's novels *Death on the Nile* (1978) and *The Mirror Crack'd* (1980)—as well as many similar books, TV shows and short stories—people die hideous deaths, but the true horror and agony of death is never shown or even mentioned. These vehicles conform to certain "family standards," wherein nothing excessively graphic is allowed and there is a stubborn, often stupid, predilection for cleaning up the murders so that no one's sensibilities are offended. The murder victim, who has been bludgeoned or stabbed or murdered in some equally ghoulish way, is usually someone everyone hated in order to increase the number of suspects and decrease the horror of the crime. Death and murder are mere *divertissements* for nosy old women or dispassionate retired inspectors with time on their hands.

This blunted, tame, TV-style approach to death and violence is sometimes considered healthier than the gut-wrenching, stomach-turning approach of contemporary shockers. But this may not be an accurate assessment. Writing about TV violence in *TV Guide*,[10] Mike Oppenheim, M.D., said, "Children can't learn to enjoy cruelty from the neat, sanitized mayhem on the average series. What they learn is far more malignant: that guns or fists are clean, efficient, exciting ways to deal with a difficult situation. . . . Real-life violence is dirty, painful, bloody, disgusting. It causes mutilation and misery, and it doesn't solve problems. It makes them worse. . . . The problem with TV violence is: it's not violent enough."

Additionally, arguments that continued exposure to horror films will have negative effects, such as desensitizing the audience to real-life violence or creating a generation of blood-lusting maniacs, appear to be unfounded. Psychoanalyst and author A.D. Hutter, in his piece "Why Violence?"[11] insists that these violent movies help us deal with our fears, give us an opportunity to relieve our tensions, "in order to do what we cannot do in our real lives—control and resolve them." He adds: "A fair amount of current research suggests that films and fiction offer a substitute or release for feelings of rage or the need for power. Certainly, the rage and insecurities of a would-be rapist are not *created* by a story, any more than a murderer is created by watching a film. In some few and very extreme cases, a killer may adopt the style of a killer he has seen or read about, but we have no evidence that fiction actually generates crime. An otherwise perfectly harmless individual doesn't see a film about rape or murder and say to himself, 'That looks interesting, I think I'll try it.' "

Horror films are also criticized as being generally tasteless and exploitative. They almost always fail to seriously explore the social problems they expose. Psychologically and emotionally disturbed individuals are rarely developed beyond their mad-slasher capabilities. Few attempts are made to understand or probe into their pathology. Horror films also tend to generate suspicion where it is often unwarranted, especially among sexual minorities. The number of movies that feature psychotic transvestites or transsexuals, for example, is legion, although such people in real life are usually guilty of nothing more heinous than being different.

This line of criticism is particularly pointless, however, because of the very nature of horror films. They must concentrate on the grotesque and unpleasant aspects of their situations and characters if they are to have any purpose at all. At least they present their assorted horrors in the right context, as a means to create terror in the audience. This is in sharp contrast to comedy programs that make fun of murder victims only days after their deaths, newspapers that run sensational headlines that are insensitive to victims and their families, and magazines that award citations to accident victims and suicides as a way of garnering chuckles.

Granted, even horror films can cross their liberal boundaries of acceptable bad taste, but often the fault lies not with the horror genre itself. Rather, it is the people who make or are in some way connected to the films who are guilty. In *Slaughter Hotel* (1973), which is about a killing spree in a sanitorium full of beautiful women, a scene toward the end has the cornered killer using a mace to rain repeated blows upon a group of nurses who are huddled together. The publicists couldn't resist using the line of ad copy, SEE THE SLASHING MASSACRE OF EIGHT INNOCENT NURSES, in order to tie in the film with the sensational murders of several young student nurses at the hands of Richard Speck. Even worse, the producer of a top television show (who once starred in a series of low-budget foreign horror pictures) admitted in an interview that he made a film in which an actual corpse, obtained from a third-world prison, was dismembered on camera.

Whatever people may think of them, modern-day shockers are certainly more vivid and exacting than they ever used to be, and it isn't likely that they will ever go back to the comparative restraint and subtlety of horror movies made in the forties. Many of those old films, such as the ones produced by Val Lewton, lacked

The thriller at its most tasteful and literate: *The Haunting.*

Another example of literate horror: *The Innocents* (with Deborah Kerr, right), based on Henry James' *The Turn of the Screw*.

visceral shocks, but made up for it with their gracious style and literacy. *I Walked With a Zombie* (1943), directed by Jacques Tourneur, is a particularly memorable example. It is an unusual, beautifully crafted melodrama about a nurse who travels to the Caribbean to care for a woman who has apparently been turned into one of the living dead. *I Walked With a Zombie* positively drips with atmosphere, fluid camera work, and interesting dialogue. There have also been a few films made after *Psycho* that are in the Val Lewton tradition, such as Robert Wise's *The Haunting* (1963) and Jack Clayton's *The Innocents* (1961). There are no severed limbs or splattered bodies on view in either film, but then both are based on excellent literary sources (the former on Shirley Jackson's *The Haunting of Hill House* and the latter on Henry James' *The Turn of the Screw*) and need no visceral embellishments.

Recent, sincere attempts to make quality horror films that lack the gory shocks today's audiences are used to (and in some cases demand) have virtually all been commercial and critical failures. Jack Clayton returned to the genre with the film version of Ray Bradbury's classic *Something Wicked This Way Comes* (1983), but the film was too insubstantial to garner support from those who appreciated the more subtle, less graphic kind of fantasy the story engendered. The film version of Peter Straub's *Ghost Story* (1981), while not as bad as the critics suggested, was also all but ruined by inconsistent direction, this time perpetrated by John Irvin. Even *The Omen* trilogy, which Straub's *Ghost Story* admirers must have considered silly and subliterate by comparison (though Straub's novel is itself not a masterpiece), showed more skill and verve on a cinematic level than many of these more "tasteful" films.

The truth is that violence, shocks, gory makeup tricks, and startling effects are, on one level at least, what horror movies are all about. Contemporary thrillers that leave out these elements will have a chance only if they substitute something

Ghost Story: Many felt this tasteful thriller didn't work.

for them—an original premise, a great script, superior direction—something that keeps the audience's mind off the fact that the obligatory shocks and gore are absent.

The horror genre will always make room for creative violence . . . its (figurative) life's blood.

How can the fantasy of movies like *The Evil Dead* compare to the horrors of the real world?

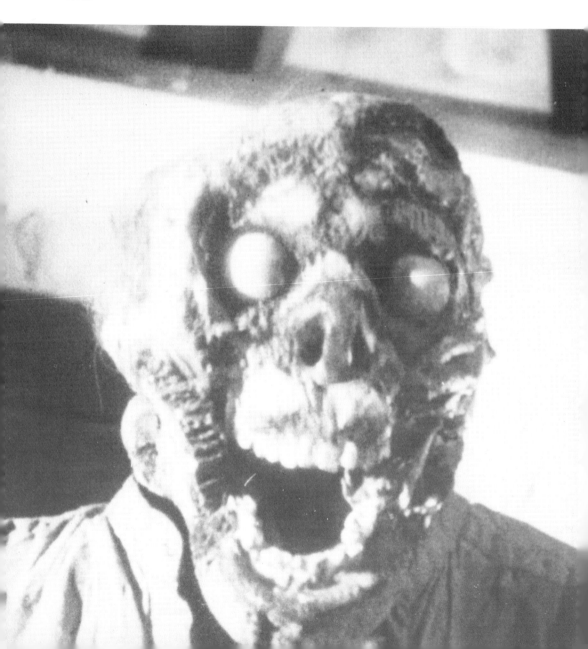

TOP SHOCKER DIRECTORS

Directors have long had a love affair with the shocker genre. No other type of picture quite allows a filmmaker to show what he can do, in cinematic terms. Shockers are films of action; often characters and dialogue are less important than what's happening physically on the screen. Many of today's filmmakers saw *Psycho* years ago and count it among their major influences. Big-time artists and low-budget schlock-makers alike, the chief ambition of many directors in the horror field is to make a picture that will blow *Psycho* out of the water, or that will at least have the kind of effect on an international audience that *Psycho* had. The fruit of such ambition is more obvious with some directors than with others.

The imaginative Canadian director David Cronenberg first came to horror film fans' attention with the release of *They Came From Within* (1976), which is sort of one part *The Tingler* and two parts Masters and Johnson. The story takes place in a self-contained apartment complex on an island off the coast of Canada. A doctor has been experimenting with parasites that would be used *in place of* actual body organs when transplants become necessary. Unfortunately, the parasite he has created, a vicious little squiggly thing about six inches in length, becomes a venereal–disease–transmitting aphrodisiac once it has infected—or literally *crawled into*—a victim. The result: The sex-crazed population starts screwing itself to death. An added complication is that the parasite not only makes people go crazy with lust but also with violence.

Through the course of the film the busy parasite wanders through halls, out of people's mouths, around distressed stomachs, and at one point, into one poor woman's vagina. Pretty soon the whole complex has been turned into a huge blood-bathed orgy. Meanwhile, the hero runs around trying to keep from being raped by the sex-hungry men and women who live there. Unfortunately, throughout the low-budget production, Cronenberg's direction is uniformly

Director David Cronenberg on the set of *Videodrome*.

uninspired. What could have been a real classic (what a plot!) is instead a cute, rather repulsive satire on our society's obsession with S E X!

In his next film, *Rabid* (1977), Cronenberg retreaded similar material with a distasteful, disturbing picture about an epidemic of rabies in and around Montreal. The cause of it all is poor Marilyn Chambers (porn star and Ivory Snow girl), who has been hospitalized after a motorcycle accident. Unaccountably, the skin graft operations on her body have produced a vagina-like organ in her underarm, from which protrudes a needle-like tongue that can drain victims of blood. Once infected, the bloodless wretches run wild in a murderous frenzy. Again, Cronenberg doesn't betray much style, but he does manage to keep the energetic and bloody proceedings moving swiftly.

It wasn't until his third film, *The Brood* (1979), that Cronenberg really started to show what he could do. It seems that disturbed mental patient Samantha Eggar (under the care of Oliver Reed, who encourages his charges to externalize

The evil "children" of *The Brood* gather for an attack.

their anxiety) has released her pent-up anger in the form of *fetuses* which grow right *on her body*. The resulting "children" are actually physical manifestations of her internal subconscious frustrations. Therefore, anyone she feels hatred for is attacked and killed by her "brood." Eggar's children run around in playsuits, jumping out of shadows and pouncing on the unsuspecting.

Cronenberg seems to have borrowed a few ideas from such diverse items as *The Forbidden Planet* and Alfred Sole's *Communion*. More stylish than its predecessors, *The Brood* showed that Cronenberg had clearly developed as a director. The murder scenes are suspenseful and well choreographed. Cinematography has improved since Cronenberg's earlier, lower-budgeted efforts. The bloodshed in *The Brood* is minimal, though some may find the ending a bit too ghoulish for their tastes. Though there's plenty of imagination and visual vividness on hand, *The Brood* still lacks that special tightness that distinguishes a really excellent product.

Cronenberg achieved real audience popularity with the heavily promoted *Scanners* (1981), which is about the battle between good and bad psychics who have rather alarming mental abilities. The advertising campaign centered on the movie's goriest sequence, in which the bad scanner (Michael Ironsides) blows up

Scanners: The "bad scanner," Michael Ironsides, about to do some more dirty work.

a good scanner's head as a demonstration of his sinister prowess. While Cronenberg gives the head-bursting scene an excellent suspense buildup (aided no doubt by the TV ad campaign, which made the scene already familiar in people's minds) it was overshadowed by the very film it was aping, Brian De Palma's *The Fury* (1978). (De Palma blew up John Cassavetes' entire *body* at the end of that one.)

As usual, *Scanners* has a lot of clever ideas, but falls short of being as good as it could have been. The acting of lead players Jennifer O'Neill and the utterly amateurish Stephen Lack (they're not kidding!) severely minimize the picture's credibility, and Cronenberg's script, while full of the requisite suspense and action, is too superficial to make *Scanners* anything more than a moment's diversion.

It was up to the special effects department to give *Scanners* its thrills, including a wonderful climactic battle of wills between Lack and Ironsides in which the two use their mental powers to play physical havoc with each other's bodies. Veins bulge, eyes sizzle and burst, flesh burns. The fight is handled so ingeniously that it is impossible to look away, no matter how gruesome it gets—and it gets very gruesome. Cronenberg keeps the film moving at a fast pace, too.

Next was *Videodrome* (1983), a disappointing movie with another excellent premise. James Woods plays a cable TV producer who accidentally picks up transmission of a program that makes his selections of porn and staged violence look provincial in comparison. The program, called "Videodrome," features nothing but unending torture and murder, all of which is *real*.

Enter Deborah Harry (lead singer of the former rock group, Blondie), who is so masochistically excited by the program that she goes to Pittsburgh—where Videodrome originates—to audition for it! Woods investigates on his own and uncovers a bizarre plot to destroy those "immoral" souls who watch the sleaze he presents on his network by frying their brains with selective TV emissions. These emissions induce brain tumors and create apparent hallucinations in the viewer. Woods imagines (or is it his imagination?) that he has developed a vagina-like orifice in the middle of his stomach that can program him like a robot when videocassettes are inserted into it!

If Cronenberg had stuck to that far-fetched but intriguing premise and played fair with the audience he would have for once come up with a film that works on every level. But he makes several mistakes. Again, he insisted on writing his own screenplay, even though he has never been able to take his admittedly excellent ideas and transform them into well-constructed properties with three-dimensional characters and well-developed story lines.

He decides to throw logic and credibility to the wind, piling up one gruesome special effects sequence after another, giving the impression that things we

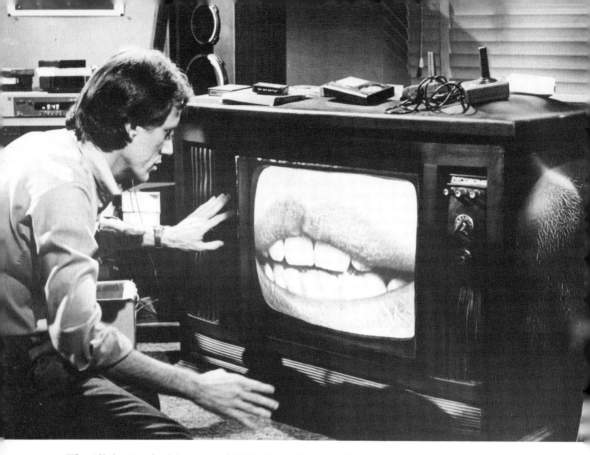

The "living" television set of *Videodrome* is a good example of David Cronenberg's erotic imagery.

thought were only Woods' hallucinations (the "vagina" in his abdomen, for instance) are real. The movie switches from a gripping suspense story to a surreal thriller to virtual fantasy, and toward the end the audience no longer cares what happens to Woods, the world, the crazy plot to warp minds with television, or much of anything else.

If none of his films up until that point had ever reached their full potential, why was Cronenberg considered an important director? Simply because the potential was there, which is not true of most of the hack directors of the stalk-the-pretty-girls-and-kill-them school. It is always possible, in any case, to overlook the flaws of Cronenberg's various movies and enjoy the man's strange, sick wit and the very imaginative touches he employs. *Videodrome*, for instance, is a cornucopia of bursting bodies, organic TV sets that breath and change shape, far-out fantasy segments, and bloodied human limbs. Cronenberg showed signs of fully appreciating the importance of well-chosen actors. In *Videodrome*, Woods and Harry, two very sensual performers, are perfect choices for the somewhat off-kilter romantic leads, and the other cast-members are all quite good.

Nonetheless, even his admirers wondered if Cronenberg would be able to rise above the capable craftsman level he had reached and become a bona fide "artist." What he needed was to turn his ideas over to accomplished, veteran screenwriters, to share his bloody visions with others—the way Hitchcock did—so that people who had the literary technique he did not have could shape his visions into more comprehensible forms. One imagines that Cronenberg thought he was coming up with something quite profound in *Videodrome*, that it was his symbolic attempt to comment on "heavy" problems of our society and its relationship to the communications media. If that was the case, the spirit was willing but the mind was weak. *Videodrome*, like all of Cronenberg's entertaining, even heartfelt attempts, is likable but pretentious. Cronenberg had shown that he could revel in assorted excesses—but could he return to the quiet, calmer style of *The Brood*, exercise restraint, and *tell a story* instead of overwhelming the audience with mere technique and offal?

And then came *The Dead Zone* (1983), a superior adaptation of Stephen King's novel about a man who comes out of a coma and finds he has the power to see into the future. In this film everything comes together beautifully—an atmospheric score by Michael Kamen, an excellent screenplay by Jeffrey Boam, and a superb lead performance from Christopher Walken, one of our best contemporary American actors (with good support from Martin Sheen). And Cronenberg's direction, perhaps because he was confident that every other element was so outstanding, is more assured than ever before.

Almost without meaning to, Cronenberg has established what we might call the "Cronenberg style." He is often referred to as someone who revels in blood and gore, and his films are indeed quite liberally graphic (and sometimes downright repulsive). There are always sexual layers to his movies, usually obvious ones, such as the vagina-like body openings in both *Rabid* and *Videodrome*, and the fact that the crazy, diseased people who inhabit Cronenberg's world are as anxious to molest one another as they are to murder. If Cronenberg can combine the strengths of *The Dead Zone* with the bizarre personal visions of his other films, the gentleman will have it *made*.

Dario Argento, an Italian thriller director, made a pretty big splash with his first release, *The Bird with the Crystal Plumage* (1969), a film that was perhaps overpraised (it was not quite as good as Hitchcock), but was not half as bad as its detractors would suggest. (See Chapter Ten for an in-depth study of this film.) Argento is one of the most stylish and enthusiastic directors working in the field today. He goes about the business of killing off his cast members—they are garroted, beheaded, crushed by car wheels, thrown in front of trains—with such relish and élan that it's positively frightening. Argento was obviously influenced

by Mario Bava, whose work he has easily surpassed. Argento usually writes or co-writes his own screenplays, which are perfectly suited to his gruesome stylistics and which never pretend to be anything but what they are—clever, compelling thriller scripts.

Argento followed up *Bird* with *Cat O' Nine Tails* (1971), a thriller that puts forth the theory that killers are the way they are because of an extra chromosome in their genetic make-up. The murderer, therefore, has to kill off everyone who knows that he has this extra chromosome. (Like many other directors who ape Hitchcock without quite absorbing the master's aplomb, Argento overdoes the wavering subjective camera from the killer's viewpoint.) Karl Malden and James Franciscus are the stars. The movie has at least two good scenes: a man pushed to his death in front of a train, and the killer's fatal plunge at the finale. Critical response was surprisingly cold, considering how well-received *Bird* was, but then *Cat O' Nine Tails* is not in its predecessor's league. It's much more violent, too, which certainly initiated a backlash from the critics.

The backlash continued with *Four Flies on Grey Velvet* (1972), which gets its title from the myth that the last thing a dead person sees remains imprinted on his lifeless eyeballs. A rock singer (Michael Brandon) finds his life and well-being threatened by an unknown maniacal killer who turns out to be his girlfriend, the toothsome Mimsy Farmer. *Four Flies* has some interesting visual touches, yet as a whole seems stagey and self-consciously directed, with tricks that call attention to themselves without being particularly effective.

Deep Red (1975), his goriest and most flamboyant shocker, was his next (and best) movie. In this chiller, David Hemmings wades through what seems (on first viewing) an almost incomprehensible script searching for the person who took an axe to his next-door neighbor—a psychic who predicted her own grisly death only hours before. While vividly detailing several more brutal murders, Argento tries to overwhelm the viewer with genuinely striking cinematography and impressive visual tricks, some of which do come off quite well. Much of the musical score is excellent, though at times the rock beat is not only out of place but so loud and irritating that the effect is almost deadening. The film is absorbing and suspenseful, occasionally tense, and sometimes unintentionally laughable. Argento has filled the picture with excellent little bits and pieces, and a particularly grotesque final scene. The killer's necklace gets caught in a descending elevator. As it begins to tighten around the woman's neck, Argento abruptly cuts to a shot of the lowering cage. The string of pearls dangles bloodily from the bottom of the elevator. Somehow this is more nauseating than had

Martin Sheen in *The Dead Zone*, Cronenberg's most accomplished film.

A victim stupidly crawls into a room full of wire to avoid the killer in Dario Argento's *Suspiria*.

Argento shown the decapitation in its entirety. It's the most ghoulishly gruesome business that Argento has ever come up with.

Susperia (1977) was Argento's next film, and here he almost managed to top *Deep Red*. Mystery and horror surround a famous dance school as the bodies pile up and women are stabbed, garroted, and brutalized in Argento's typically grotesque but poetic fashion. Those with a tolerance for this sort of thing will be disappointed only by a lackluster, plodding final quarter, but everyone can thrill to Argento's stylish visual touches and the eerily effective electronic music by Goblin. Certain sequences in *Susperia*, as in *Deep Red*, are really charged with directorial brilliance and energy—for instance, a savage double slaying near the beginning, and a gross infestation of maggots later on—but in the long run these imaginative parts are better than the whole. Joan Bennett plays the role of the head of the school as if she were still toiling in that awful old soap opera, "Dark Shadows."

Argento's films have a sadistic, somewhat misogynistic streak to them (he also usually includes some stereotyped homosexual character who winds up getting killed as much for his sexual orientation as for the sake of any plot twist), but it seems more an expression of his bizarre compulsions than an attempt to attack women or humankind in general. His more recent films excel in sumptuous lighting effects, beautiful sets, and some remarkable (if gaudy) interior art direction. At his best, Argento is a craftsman of dazzling skill; at his worst, he's boring. In any case, he exhibits more genuine flair and talent than any ten "stalk-and-slash" directors put together.

His films after *Suspiria*—*Inferno, Tenebrae,* and *Phenomena*—have yet to be released in the U.S. as of early 1985, though plans are afoot to finally do so. The fact that his first film, *Bird with the Crystal Plumage*, was re-released in 1982 (as *Phantom of Terror*) indicates that there is still much interest in the Argento product. Argento also worked on the soundtrack of George Romero's gory opus, *Dawn of the Dead* (1979).

Brian De Palma has been accused of being a mere Hitchcock imitator, someone so enamored of *Psycho* and Hitchcock's other pictures that he can't do anything but rework those old movies and film them in what he feels is the style of "the master." Actually, De Palma's films really aren't like Hitchcock's or anyone else's; as he has said, the worst he can be accused of is using some of the filmic "grammar" suggested and perfected by the master of suspense. And when De Palma's best films are compared to those of his competitors, you can readily see that there's something to be said for being "grammatically" correct.

De Palma's first big thriller was *Sisters* (1973), a "deranged twin" melodrama starring Margot Kidder as a zesty French psychopath. It was clearly influenced by *Psycho*. *Sisters* (which is fully analyzed in Chapter Ten) got De Palma off to a good start, but he followed it up, unfortunately, with *Obsession* (1976), a poorly conceived homage to Hitchcock's *Vertigo*, and with other films that do not quite fall into the scope of this book.

De Palma's *Carrie* (1976), however, is one of the most accomplished horror films of the decade. He skillfully and lovingly fashioned a superb chiller based on Stephen King's excellent first novel about a high-school girl, Carrie White, who takes revenge on her callous classmates by unleashing her psychic powers at the prom. Performances (particularly Sissy Spacek as Carrie) and cinematography are of the highest caliber, and Pino Donaggio's score is memorable. Though not as moving or (literally) explosive as the book, *Carrie* is packed with visual intensity. De Palma gets carried away at times with his affection for (or affec*tation*

Director Brian De Palma on the set of *Body Double*.

Carrie White (Sissy Spacek) is drenched with pig's blood on the night of the senior prom in De Palma's *Carrie*.

of) slow motion and splitscreens, though such devices are used quite effectively in most instances. Perhaps the highlight of this film, which has many outstanding sequences, is the death of Carrie's mother (Piper Laurie). Carrie telekinetically animates all the cutlery in the kitchen and causes it to fly across the room, puncture the mother's body, and pin her to the wall in a macabre imitation of the crucifix Carrie is forced to pray to for hours on end when her mother locks her up in the closet.

De Palma's follow-up to *Carrie, The Fury* (1978), is an extremely uneven thriller about government forces tracking down and exploiting two teenagers who have psychic abilities. The plot centers on Kirk Douglas' attempts to find his psychic teenage son (Andrew Stevens)—who has been kidnapped by the government for use as a weapon—with the aid of a young woman (Amy Irving) who can make people start bleeding by touching them. (There are numerous nauseating scenes of people hemorrhaging.) The film has mutiple flaws, including long, dull shots that pan back and forth during conversations, and a lot of sequences simply land with a thud.

But in the midst of this De Palma returns, sporadically, to his virtuosity, peppering the sloppy film with a variety of technical and visual highlights; these seem to be the director's way of flexing his muscles and strutting. A particularly memorable scene occurs when Andrew Stevens uses his psychic abilities to whip head-villainess Fiona Lewis up off the floor (her rigid body just snaps up from the carpet in what has to be a cleverly reversed shot), where he had knocked her moments before, and then levitates her several feet above the ground before spinning her around at such speed that her blood, as one critic puts it, "starts painting the wallpaper." There's no question that *The Fury* is excessive and self-indulgent, but it grows on you in spite of its imperfections.

Despite its general silliness and its sleazy exploitation of transsexualism, *Dressed to Kill* (1980), De Palma's next movie, is a well-crafted crackerjack thriller that works almost every step of the way. Still under the influence of Hitchcock's *Psycho*, De Palma came up with a nail-biting suspense film, and his best work since *Carrie*. The story deals with a financially astute high-class hooker (Nancy Allen) and a teenager (Keith Gordon) who team up to track down the maniac who murdered the boy's mother (Angie Dickinson). Of course, the plot is as dubious and inane as most psychosexual shockers, but at least this handsomely mounted production is done with style and finesse. An elevator razor-slashing scene—the film's equivalent to *Psycho*'s shower murder (though not on its level)—is handled by De Palma in his own inimitable manner, without directly aping Hitchcock.

For the first time since *Carrie*, De Palma shows restraint and wisdom in regard to his use of splitscreens and slow-motion sequences. The ending of the elevator murder is stretched out to near-unbearable tension. There are many taut sequences and sexy moments, and an amusing scene on the subway when Allen is pursued not only by the killer but also by a gang of slobbering hoodlums. Dickinson's encounter with a handsome gentleman in the Museum of Modern Art—which ends in an improbable but enjoyable sexual encounter in the back of a taxi cab—is a good example of the smouldering eroticism on display in many of De Palma's pictures. There are no hidden meanings in *Dressed to Kill*; it is not a moral fable, simply a polished, well-executed horror film. (For the angry feminist reaction to *Dressed to Kill*, see Chapter Four.)

Blow Out (1981), about a movie soundman who inadvertently witnesses the assassination of a presidential candidate in a Chappaquidick-like incident while out one night recording sound effects, is noteworthy on two counts. First, the soundman (John Travolta) happens to work on horror pictures of the cheesy, stalk-and-slash type that De Palma himself has such contempt for. De Palma uses this to open the film with a take-off on such movies. In the beginning, the camera becomes the eyes of a stalking psycho as he wanders around a dormitory staring into windows and finally cornering one poor girl—in the shower room, naturally. But when she opens her mouth to scream, the sound that comes out is such a pitiful squawk that the director can only tear his hair in frustration. It's Travolta's job to dub in a better scream, and the cynical, ironic ending has him using the actual death rattle of Nancy Allen, with whom he has become involved, on the soundtrack.

The second interesting element is the subplot of a hired killer (John Lithgow) who strangles a couple of Nancy Allen look-alikes so that when he murders Allen herself, everyone will think it was the work of a sex maniac, and not part of some conspiracy. Unfortunately, these sex-crime slayings are gratuitous and only moderately effective. The fact that Allen is directed to play the woman in a dumb-bunny, nitwit manner makes the film seem misogynous.

Although *Blow Out* is engrossing, it is undermined by one-dimensional characters and poor motivation. De Palma's tricks seem tiresome and often fall flat. The picture even lacks the handsome look of *Dressed to Kill*. Pino Donaggio's score is equally uninspired.

De Palma's next film was a remake of the gangster flick *Scarface*. It falls outside the scope of this book, but was attacked because of a bloody chainsaw killing (most of which is actually off camera).

De Palma regained lost ground with his next film, *Body Double* (1984), which infuriated feminists and critics, but delighted the moviemaker's many admirers. Craig Wasson plays a struggling actor who house-sits a futuristic apartment for an acquaintance who suggests that Wasson use the telescope to watch a beautiful neighbor (Deborah Shelton) do her nightly erotic dance. Wasson becomes

Deborah Shelton and Craig Wasson watch a thief make off with the lady's purse in *Body Double*, De Palma's 1984 thriller.

infatuated with the lady and follows her around, but is soon alarmed to realize that a much more sinister figure is apparently stalking her. He watches helplessly through the telescope as this other man breaks into the lady's apartment. Eventually he murders her with a gigantic power drill, in spite of Wasson's efforts to save her. (This scene is very exciting and well-edited, without being overly graphic.) Suspecting that he has been an innocent dupe in a murder plot, Wasson invades the world of erotic movies in order to question another woman (Melanie Griffith) whom he thinks may have played a part in his neighbor's horrible death.

Body Double isn't successful on every level but it is absorbing, a literal materialization of De Palma's bizarre artistic obsessions. Pino Donaggio's music is provocative, constantly flowing with and embellishing the movie's many different moods. The only scene that really doesn't work apes the "revolving camera" Hitchcock used during the famous James Stewart–Kim Novak kiss in *Vertigo*. It serves to make actors Wasson and Shelton look ridiculous. Despite this, *Body Double* is a kick and a half, one of the most entertaining thrillers in a long, long time.

Tobe Hooper is usually lumped in with Cronenberg, Argento and De Palma as a "horror master," in spite of the fact that his output has been comparatively limited. His reputation rests mostly on his first picture, *The Texas Chainsaw Massacre* (1974). (For a detailed analysis of that film, and why it had such an impact, see Chapter Ten.) His style is as different from the first three directors' discussed in this chapter as their styles are from one another's.

Tobe Hooper's classic shocker: *Texas Chainsaw Massacre.*

Hooper has not yet topped *Chainsaw*, in spite of bigger budgets and increasing mainstream exposure. His second film, most widely released under the title *Eaten Alive* (1976), takes place at an isolated hotel where guests are systematically slaughtered by the proprietor (a scythe-wielding maniac) and then fed to his pet alligator. The only time the film comes alive is in the last few minutes—as thrilling as *Chainsaw's* finale—when Hooper frenetically intercuts the alligator's pursuit of a little girl in the hotel's crawlspace with the proprietor's murderous charge toward his two latest victims.

Hooper also directed the TV-movie version of Stephen King's bestseller *Salem's Lot* (1979), but TV is such a bad place in general for horror movies that it's impossible to discern whether the weakness of the film (about a vampire infestation in modern-day New England) was Hooper's fault or the CBS censor's. His next offering was a theatrical film entitled *The Funhouse* (1981), about a group of kids pursued by a maniac in the title location. Although a paperback novelization of the screenplay, written by Owen West, indicated a rather interesting story line with many novel developments, supporting characters, and a good suspenseful buildup to the main event, most of this was dropped in favor of a simplistic "divide and murder" movie, all other elements of the screenplay jettisoned in favor of an expanded version of the climactic sequence (the teenagers being stalked in the funhouse). Possibly intimidated by the larger budget and the large-screen format, Hooper crafted only a few good moments (such as an amusing *Psycho* parody at the beginning). The end product is largely forgettable.

Hooper was to have directed *Venom*, but was replaced early in the picture. Luckily he jumped immediately into the Steven Spielberg production of *Poltergeist* (1982), a well-received, well-done tale of a surburban household beset by devils, demons, and lively, unearthed corpses. The picture should have been a feather in his directorial cap, but unfortunately the rumor started that Spielberg himself guided most of the action, which was patently unfair (as anyone who had seen *Texas Chainsaw* realized). Hooper's next film was the exciting, notable thriller *Lifeforce* (1985). Hooper's future projects to date include: a remake of *Invaders of Mars*; a big-screen version of Marvel Comics' *Spider-Man*; and of course, *Texas Chainsaw Massacre Two*.

There have been many top directors who have dabbled in the horror genre without making it their life's work. Before directing the homosexual multiple-murder thriller, *Cruising* (see Chapter Five), William Friedkin soared to the top with the film version of William Peter Blatty's *The Exorcist*. It was the killer-fish epic, *Jaws*, that put Steven Spielberg (*E.T., Raiders of the Lost Ark*) on the map. The

Tobe Hooper jumped into the big time when he directed the Steven Spielberg production of *Poltergeist*.

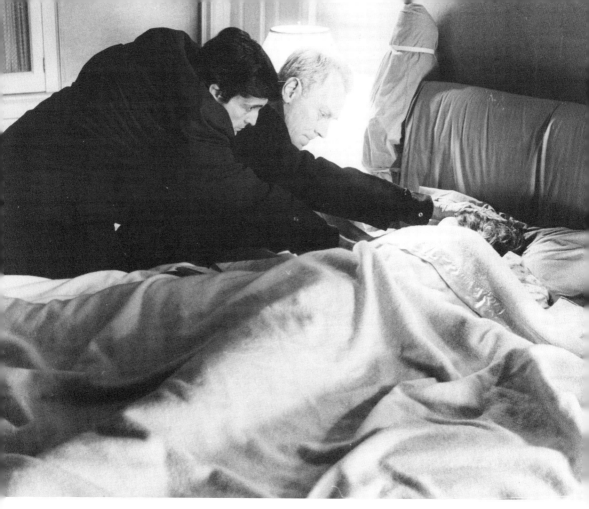

The priests watch over the sleeping figure of the possessed little girl in *The Exorcist*.

prestigious Stanley Kubrick tried his hand in the genre—only once, mercifully—with the disappointing adaptation of Stephen King's *The Shining*. Robert Altman, Peter Bogdanovich, and Sidney Lumet have also tried their hands at the genre.

Looking at it now, it's hard to remember that at one time *The Exorcist* (1973) was a fresh and novel idea. The shots of flying furniture, the gory makeup and trick effects, the theme of demonic possession in youngsters were all on vivid display for the first time in Friedkin's movie. Now there have been so many imitations (and imitations of imitations) that all the original elements seem time-worn and a trifle dated. In fact, *The Exorcist*, with its disjointed, choppy continuity, now seems like a rather tedious movie, into which parts of a more skillfully crafted thriller have been spliced.

The reason for *The Exorcist*'s hybrid quality is simply that the movie is not one that can stand the test of time. Admittedly, it was a trendsetter and a groundbreaker in many ways, and its good spots—its many visually exciting sequences—are extremely effective. But a lot of the film, particularly the expository scenes between the shocks, are routinely directed and flat and dull to watch. Perhaps the problem is that *The Exorcist* takes itself too seriously. The story of a little girl who is possessed by a demon, and who turns into a hideous, homicidal piece of festering evil that nothing short of an exorcism can cure, is hardly grand opera, after all. In some ways, John Boorman's sequel, *Exorcist Two: The Heretic* (1977), despite its incomprehensible screenplay, is a more entertaining and certainly more beautiful movie to look at.

Jaws (1975) was a trendsetter, too, initiating a second cycle of monster movies, the likes of which had not been seen since the mid-fifties (when all manner of voracious bugs and mammals paraded across the screen in pursuit of terrified

The killer shark of *Jaws* is about to munch on some unlucky swimmer.

humans). In fact, *Jaws* is really just an updated version of those old fifties movies, though few of those pictures were handled with the flair and expertise of this exciting and suspenseful chiller.

Jaws may be a thrilling and innovative horror film, but it is also cold-blooded and distasteful, making rather shallow comments about human nature and leaving a rather bad aftertaste. *Jaws* is considered a quality film for many reasons—Spielberg's direction, the big budget, the popular (and rather terrible) best-selling novel it was based on, and Roy Scheider's portrayal of the sheriff/ protagonist. Scheider plays an ordinary man, not a superhero. Unfortunately, the film lacks sensitivity and compassion, and in that regard is more in line with horror pictures that are meant to be gross and cynical.

The most heartbreaking scene in *Jaws* is when the little boy on the float is attacked by the shark and his mother is confronted with the shredded, washed up, empty float on the beach afterwards. This is perhaps the only time when there is any attempt to generate pathos, although the usual audience reaction is one of mildly disgusted giggles. *Jaws* is a technically proficient movie, to be sure, but it isn't any work of art.

Robert Altman has made at least two films that fit into unconventional psycho-thriller molds. The first is *That Cold Day in the Park* (1969), a bizarre story with Sandy Dennis as a spinster who takes in a handsome young man (Michael Burns) who is pretending to be mute. She imprisons the boy and supplies his every need, including a prostitute, whom she goes out and drags home for Burns' pleasure. The final sequence has the crazed Dennis stabbing the woman to death in a jealous pique. The film is full of sick passion of a sort, but is utterly devoid of feeling.

Images (1972) is considered by some to be Altman's version of Roman Polanski's *Repulsion*. Altman's heroine, played by Susannah York, has hallucinations wherein her past lovers, both dead and alive, come back to haunt her. She decides that the only way to get rid of a phantom is to kill it. So she does. Unfortunately, sometimes these "phantoms" are *real*. Altman's approach to the violence of the film is without subtlety. In one scene a victim is stabbed in the chest just as he pulls his sweater up over his face (to hide the gadgetry no doubt), and a gush of spurting blood spouts out from his body with the force of a firehose. Blood may spurt that way in real life, perhaps, but somehow the scene doesn't look as realistic as intended. *Images* has good scenes, is more ambitious than the usual thriller, and is fairly effective as an exercise in "pure cinema," but it's far too uneven to be as memorable as it could have been (an old song where the self-indulgent Altman is concerned). His 1979 thriller, *Quintet*, a futuristic story of weird games and murders, with Paul Newman, was not well-received by the critics or public.

Peter Bogdanovich, the director of the brilliant drama, *The Last Picture Show*, and many others, started out with a notable horror effort, *Targets* (1968). It made a disturbing corollary between real-life horror and the horror of the movies. Set mostly at a drive-in theater, the movie is about a deranged sniper picking off members of an audience watching an old-time horror film. It was the last movie for Boris Karloff, who plays an aging horror star making an appearance at the outdoor theater. Most critics considered it a poignant farewell for him and an outstanding debut for director Bogdanovich, who also appears in the picture.

Stanley Kubrick, the very gifted director of such films as *Dr. Strangelove* and *Paths of Glory*, made one ill-advised foray into the horror genre with *The Shining* (1980). Kubrick labored for years on this weary exercise in the macabre, while other, lesser-known directors had produced dozens of horror films that were more frightening and creatively engineered. Instead of fretting over the editing of his "masterpiece," Kubrick should have left the house from time to time to check out what was happening in the genre. Even a 99¢ item like *Friday the 13th* was scarier and more energetic.

Faced with the prospect of admitting that *The Shining* was a tedious film that merely made a mess of King's classy, terrifying best-seller, his proponents suggested that Kubrick's adaptation was fraught with heavy meanings and deep symbolic statements (as opposed to mere cheap shocks). Unfortunately, none of these critics were able to tell exactly what these intellectual undertones *were*. Isn't *The Shining* simply a story of an alcoholic writer who brings his family to stay with him while he maintains a huge haunted resort emptied for the winter? Isn't it merely a psychological ghost story? Kubrick should have accepted the material at face value and not tried to obfuscate its considerable escapist entertainment value.

The Shining is constructed so poorly that scenes and meanings are jumbled, characterizations are shredded, and potentially socko sequences are virtually thrown away. Long, long takes and repetitious shots serve only to detach the audience when they should be excited and involved. Kubrick makes so many mistakes throughout the course of the film that it is painful to watch. He inserted so many flashforwards depicting a tidal wave of blood rushing from the elevators (what an image!) that when the actual event finally occurs late in the picture, whatever shock value it might have had has already been dissipated. The scene wherein Jack Nicholson chops down the bathroom door and shouts, "Here's Johnny!" is static and laughable. Even the sequence in which Nicholson chases little Danny Lloyd through the maze is a wash-out; Kubrick merely switches back and forth from the same two or three viewpoints, resisting any effort to present the chase in more excitingly cinematic terms. It's as if Kubrick sabotaged his own work simply so that no one would accuse him of directing a *mere* horror film. But instead of doing something genuinely profound and different, Kubrick didn't even deliver the goods on the most basic, visceral level. The film version of *The Shining* removes the guts from the novel, and doesn't replace them with anything. Even King's literate characterizations and observations were mostly jettisoned.

Stanley Kubrick is a talented and interesting director, but his work has been very inconsistent. *A Clockwork Orange* and *2001: A Space Odyssey* garnered positive critical reaction. *The Shining*, however, didn't fool anyone. Horror is not the genre for every director. Only those who have an instinctive feel for it, who know what's being done by others in the field and can project the proper mood, style, and approach to the material, should ever attempt a horror film.

Foreign directors have also tried their hand at making Hitchcock–inspired opuses and other types of shockers, especially the French *auteurs* François Truffaut and Claude Chabrol. Inexplicably, perhaps because they fondly remember his earlier, autobiographical films about Antoine Doinel (which were evocative if overrated), the critics always greeted Truffaut's thrillers with acclaim. But *The Bride Wore Black* (1967), which features a chubby Jeanne Moreau running about killing her husband's murderers, is perhaps the most pathetic homage to the master of suspense ever conceived. From a technical standpoint, Traffaut's action sequences are downright amateurish. Since technique and cutting were always so important to Hitchcock, it seems incredible that anyone would label this travesty "Hitchcockian." Bernard Herrmann's excellent score is wasted on a truly pitiable movie.

Claude Chabrol's thrillers, while not masterpieces, are miles ahead of Truffaut's. Chabrol used Anthony Perkins in *The Champagne Murders* (1967), about skullduggery in France's wine country, and again later in *Ten Day's Wonder* (1972). *This Man Must Die* (1969) is a well-photographed revenge-theme picture that borders a bit too much on camp. *Le Boucher* (1971), which was very well received upon its release in the United States, is a rather haunting (if imperfect) story about a schoolteacher's relationship with a troubled mass murderer.

Chabrol's *Wedding in Blood* (1973) is another uneven mystery, but it does boast a tense sequence leading up to a brutal clubbing murder on a highway, as well as a rich atmosphere and an excellent musical score. Other Chabrol thrillers include *Just Before Nightfall* and *Dirty Hands*. In spite of all the thrillers he has done, perhaps Chabrol's finest films are actually his early psychological studies, such as *Les Bonnes Femmes*, which has a climactic murder, but is not a traditional shocker by any means. Rather, it is a poignant, grim, and macabre study of romantic despair and disillusionment, and one of the French cinema's minor masterpieces.

The famous Swedish director Ingmar Bergman has turned to the horror field (in his own way) a number of times during his career. *The Virgin Spring* (1960) is a rape-and-revenge drama. *The Hour of the Wolf* (1968) is about a man haunted by the apparitions he sees on an isolated island. *Persona* (1966) contains some truly horrifying images in its dissection of the relationship between a patient and her nurse. *The Passion of Anna* (1969) concerns the troubled inhabitants of an island, one of whom performs acts of cruelty and mutilation on animals. Bergman's themes are far deeper and more thought-provoking (and sometimes more pretentious) than those of the average "mad slasher" movie.

While no one would consider any of the following directors among the world's finest, these "second stringers" are lifted above the rabble either by virtue of their prolific output in the genre, by style or craftsmanship, or by the fact that they have a large number of devoted followers.

The late Mario Bava deserves mention for no other reason than *Blood and Black Lace* (1964), an important shocker that is discussed in depth in Chapter Ten. But this visual stylist and Italian trendsetter made a great many other horror films, including supernatural works (*Black Sunday*/1961); anthology films (*Black Sabbath*/1963); science fiction chillers (*Planet of the Vampires*/1965); and shockers such as the tepid *The Evil Eye* (1962), the inept *Hatchet for the Honeymoon* (1970), and the rousing axe-murder epic *Twitch of the Death Nerve* (1971). At their best, Bava's movies are exquisitely lighted and photographed and often drenched with low-budget imagination and atmosphere. At their worst (*Beyond the Door Part Two*/1979), they are tedious and atrocious.

Another prolific fan-favorite is the late Terence Fisher who, along with Freddie Francis, directed dozens upon dozens of those abysmal Frankenstein, Dracula, and other assorted horror films in the late fifties and afterwards for Britain's Hammer and Amicus Film Studios. Aside from a couple of interesting items, such as *Island of Terror* (1966) and *Island of the Burning Doomed* (1973), the man's output was generally amusing but worthless. Meanwhile Mr. Francis is also responsible for *Paranoiac* and a bizarre item entitled *Mumsy Nanny Sonny and Girly* (1970) about an entire family of psychopaths who play disgusting games like putting heads in pots on the stove and boiling them.

Curtis Harrington, besides directing some "aging actress" films in the seventies (see Chapter Eight), came out with *Games* (1967), an inferior *Diabolique* imitation which also stars Simone Signoret; *The Killing Kind* (1973), about yet another mother-dominated son who has homicidal inclinations, considered by some to be Harrington's highwater mark; and *Ruby* (1977), a truly awful picture about a series of supernatural murders at a drive-in theater. He also directed many made-for-TV thrillers. Some people take Harrington far more seriously than he

Director Curtis Harrington (center) on the set of *Who Slew Auntie Roo?* with film reporters Lawrence J. Quirk (left) and Frank Leyendecker in 1971 at Shepperton Studios, England.

deserves; parts of his films are inevitably better than the whole. (Harrington now directs some segments of the TV show, *Dynasty*, which is a horror of a different kind.)

Wes Craven began to cut a notch for himself with *The Last House on the Left* (1972), which featured the popular ad slogan KEEP TELLING YOURSELF—IT'S ONLY A MOVIE! The first part of the film unflinchingly details the capture, humiliation, rape, and murder of two teen-aged girls at the hands of a gang of vicious, callous creeps. The second half shows how the girls' parents get revenge, including scenes when the father uses a chainsaw on one man, and the mother castrates another with her teeth and then kicks the living daylights out of his female companion. It's the violence that counts in this film, not the allegory (the film is alleged to be based on Bergman's *Virgin Spring*), but, although fairly crude and slap-dash, the emotional, physical power of the movie is undeniable.

Craven's follow-ups include the abysmal *The Hills Have Eyes* (1977), about a family of travelers versus pathological mountain folk (a popular theme in books and movies of the seventies) and *Deadly Blessing* (1982), about how a beautiful young widow in a Hittite community must contend with the hostility of her neighbors and a series of murders attributed to a maniac or "incubus." Since *Deadly Blessing* is far better than the usual run-of-the-mill stalk-and-slasher, it's too bad that Craven was unable to make it as good as it could have been.

Craven's best film to date is *A Nightmare on Elm Street* (1984), about a group of teenagers who all have the same dream, in which an awful-looking maniac with razors on his fingers pursues them through the darkness. They come to realize that if the maniac kills them in their dreams, they won't be waking up! This bizarre, energetic, imaginative and rather creepy terror film has a clever script (flawed by a ridiculous ending), many startling and horrifying scenes, and some truly excellent special effects. Unfortunately, Craven still lacks that certain directorial finesse that would make his films really top-notch.

Although he also directed the interesting *Demon* and the schlocky *Q*, Larry Cohen's main contribution to the horror genre is a zesty little item entitled *It's Alive* (1974), which features perhaps the most unusual homicidal maniac in screen history—a newborn human baby! Of course this little fellow is a bit out of the ordinary; he was born with claws and fangs and kills off everyone in the operating room except his horrified mother (Sharon Farrell), then crawls away to terrorize—yes, terrorize—the city. *It's Alive* is not nearly as absurd or as laughable as it sounds, due to Cohen's tense direction and Bernard Herrmann's ominous, evocative musical score, and the wise decision to show only glimpses of the mutant marauding baby as it kills milkmen and other hapless parties. *It's Alive* was so successful that Cohen made an entertaining but inferior sequel, *It Lives Again*, in 1978, which has *three* killer infants on the prowl.

The prolific Peter Sasdy's *The Devil Within Her* (1975), with Joan Collins, is also about a killer infant, this one possessed by the malevolent spirit of an evil dwarf, but the picture is truly idiotic, failing to avoid virtually every pitfall. For one thing, the baby is physically normal, not the long-toothed horror of Cohen's melodrama, making its killing spree (it decapitates poor Donald Pleasance with a shovel at one point) seem totally implausible.

Before hitting the (relative) big time with his *Porky's* movies, Bob Clark turned out a couple of interesting horror films. *Deathdream* (1972), is one of a handful of horror movies that include social commentary, characterization, and depth along with the *de rigueur* thrills and chills. It's a disturbing, violent fantasy about a soldier who comes home to his family, *after* they have received news of his death, and who is eventually responsible for a series of ghastly murders. The film is sort of an allegory about shell-shocked and shattered young men who have become immune to the horrible effects of violence, and on that level is truly tragic and memorable.

Clark also made *Black Christmas* (a.k.a. *Stranger in the House*/1975), which takes place in a sorority house whose girls are terrified by obscene phone calls, a mysterious killer, and several brutal murders. There are a few too many tepid scenes, but overall the picture has a stylish look and Clark makes good use of an atmospheric subjective camera.

George Romero helped bring about a new graphic realism in screen violence with his "classic" *Night of the Living Dead* in 1968, then carried it to what he calls

The zombies of *Night of the Living Dead* on the rampage.

"comic book" extremes in sequels *Dawn of the Dead* and *Day of the Dead*. *Night of the Living Dead* details what happens when radiation blanketing the earth causes corpses to rise from graves and autopsy tables and hunt down and devour the living. The film has a butchershop ambience, brought about by Romero's insistence on substituting sausages for human limbs and entrails, so that the zombies can have something to munch on. It quickly became a popular cult item, though not everyone was thrilled. One critic said: "Wait until you're dead to see it."

Night of the Living Dead is actually more frightening by reputation than it is in reality, but it does have a few brilliantly horrific (and poignant) moments and a lot of spooky atmosphere. The basic premise is a veritable cornucopia of horror piled on top of horror.

The opening scene at the cemetery, when the heroine (Judith O'Dea) and her brother are attacked by the silent, slow-moving zombie, is all the more terrifying because it takes place in broad daylight. O'Dea escapes from the zombies, but has to leave her brother behind. Later, when she and several others are hiding out in an abandoned country house, she hears a radio report about the zombies' behavior. Romero alternates shots of the radio and O'Dea's face, moving closer to the girl and radio as he cuts back and forth. When the radio announcer mentions the zombies' penchant for eating human flesh, we can tell from the look on O'Dea's face that she is thinking about her brother and what must have happened to him. It's a very disturbing moment.

After directing several more low-budget horror/suspense items (*The Crazies*, *Martin*, and a non-horror film entitled *Knightriders*) Romero achieved some kind of mainstream respectability by teaming up with writer Stephen King on *Creepshow* (1981), an anthology film inspired by the old EC comic books (but with King's original stories). Underground gore met high-budget production values and serious actors (Viveca Lindfors, E.G. Marshall, Hal Holbrook). Stephen King also made his acting debut in the film, playing a farmer who contracts a creepy green fungus, which covers his entire body. Other stories feature a human head as a birthday cake, two lovers who get revenge on the man who drowned them, and a horrible monster in a packing crate who kills a shrewish wife. Perhaps the best segment is the one with the horde of ugly, pernicious roaches that bedevil E.G. Marshall.

Some critics and fans discuss Romero and his "dead" movies as if he were Fellini and his pictures on a par with *La Dolce Vita*. *Dawn of the Dead*, for instance, was hyped (*overhyped*, like *Halloween*) as a spoof of consumerism, and much was made of the way the zombies cluster around a shopping mall because it had been "an important part of their lives" when they were living. Rather than imbuing them with dubious symbolism, Romero's films should simply be taken as entertaining, (usually) well-edited action/gore pictures.

Viveca Lindfors looks as if she's giving her opinion of the recent films she's been cast in. This shot is taken from George Romero's *Creepshow*.

BLOOD WITH (SOME) RESTRAINT

Many of the horror films made in the early sixties were unabashed (and inferior) copies of Hitchcock's *Psycho*, but this is not representative of all horror-movie trends after 1960. In many ways the sixties and earlier seventies were a latter-day golden age of horror, a time when there was still a reasonable, comparative amount of restraint depicted in both theme and the use of graphic violence, though, as we shall see, the seeds were being planted (particularly in low-budget independent films) for the gorier splatter-movies and ultraviolent epics of the late seventies and eighties.

One of the most amusing (and rather bizarre) trends was the "aging actress" phenomena. Although the killer in *Psycho* was revealed at the end to be a young man in his mother's clothing, for most of the length of the picture early audiences thought a batty middle-aged lady was the murderer. The next step was to make the batty middle-aged lady the murderer. A lot of stars of the movies' golden age found themselves cast in lurid melodramas and axe-murder movies, if for no other reason than it was the only kind of work they were offered. Male stars such as John Wayne were still playing heroic "macho" roles, still romancing women (in the movies, that is) who were often no older than their female counterparts had been back in the forties, in spite of the fact that Wayne and his peers were themselves a bit long in the tooth. But this time-in-stasis approach didn't work for the women, who were forced to give the romantic parts to younger actresses while they found few roles other than those in horror films. Male actors were "middle-aged" and had faces full of "character." Female stars were merely "aging."

The film that got this trend off to a start was *Whatever Happened to Baby Jane?* (1962), based on the novel by Henry Farrell. It features the team-up of two legendary movie greats, Bette Davis and Joan Crawford, in a horrific, often hilarious horror show about two sister has-beens, their sibling rivalry and sado-masochistic relationship in a crumbling mansion outside Hollywood. The classic film is a real oddity, but a very entertaining one, with two knockout perform-ances and many excellent sequences, particularly one in which Davis, cornering Crawford as she tries to phone outside for assistance, kicks her crippled sister repeatedly in the back and stomach. There's also a nifty scene when Davis brains a maid who's trying to help Crawford escape. Robert Aldrich's direction is adequate, though not topnotch, and not as effective as the performances of the leading ladies (particularly Davis').

The story line hinges on an early scene, wherein it is suggested that Crawford's disability was brought about when the jealous Davis—whose career was on the wane—ran her car into Crawford while Crawford opened the gate to their driveway. But at the very end of the picture Crawford reveals that it was *she* who was driving the car, and an inebriated Davis who was opening the gate—Crawford tried to run over her sister. "You mean all this time we could have been friends?" drawls Davis as sister Blanche (Crawford) expires on the beach. This doesn't make the slightest bit of sense; if anything, "Baby Jane" (Davis) would have treated her sister even more sadistically and contemptuously had she remembered that Blanche had been trying to kill her that night, and would not have wasted a second doing anything but rubbing it into her how her murderous attempt had backfired. But then, we can hardly expect logic from anyone as crazy as "Baby Jane" Hudson.

The picture was an enormous success, and both Crawford and Davis found their careers revitalized. Soon both were starring in a series of *Baby Jane* imitations, spin-offs, and offspring.

Davis went immediately into *Dead Ringer* (1964), a nominal shocker co-starring Peter Lawford, and directed by her old *Now, Voyager* co-star, Paul Henried. The film was largely forgettable, but does have several interesting aspects: Davis plays twins, the poorer of whom murders the wealthier and takes her place, much to boyfriend Lawford's confusion; Andre Previn's opening theme music is quite evocative and stunning, much better than the movie deserves; and Peter Lawford's death at the hands of a snarling, tearing, voracious Great Dane is rather energetic. There are also a few clever plot twists for Davis fans to enjoy.

Davis' next thriller project was *Hush . . . Hush, Sweet Charlotte* (1965), in which she was to be reteamed with Joan Crawford (who bowed out due to "illness," necessitating the signing of Olivia de Havilland) and director Robert Aldrich. *Hush . . . Hush* plays like a dark, macabre version of the old romantic movies most of its stars used to appear in. The screenplay is basically an unconvincing but adequate reworking of *Diabolique* (with some excellent dialogue, however), a plot that serves to further victimize a batty old woman (Davis) who years ago was unfairly accused of cutting off the head and hands of

Bette Davis faces her most formidable opponent—herself—in *Dead Ringer*.

her lover (Bruce Dern). Performances by Davis (who is completely convincing as the pathetic, pixilated Charlotte), Agnes Moorehead, Cecil Kellaway, Mary Astor, and Joseph Cotten are excellent, but the real scene-stealer is Olivia de Havilland, who, in a role that is almost the flip side of her Miss Melanie in *Gone With the Wind*, gives a villainous performance that builds in intensity and flair without any false notes or gratuitous histrionics.

The film's shock sequences—heads rolling down staircases, severed hands laying about, bodies coming back from the grave—are reasonably effective, if corny by today's standards. Ultimately, *Hush . . . Hush* is a diabolical story of revenge and rage and festering bitterness, with an atmosphere and tone that suggest eeriness and sorrow without wallowing in them. The axe murder of Bruce Dern, which occurs in the prologue, was fairly bloody for the time, and elicited some negative reaction. Agnes Moorehead's death (de Havilland bats her with a chair and sends her hurtling down the stairs) and the climactic deaths of de Havilland and Cotten as they toast their good fortune (Davis pushes a huge stone planter atop their heads) are very well-handled.

Davis also appeared in *The Nanny, The Anniversary, Burnt Offerings*, and other thrillers during the sixties/early seventies, none of which really fall into the scope of this book.

Meanwhile, Crawford appeared in *The Caretakers* (1963), another nominal thriller set in a mental hospital, as a head nurse named Lucretia Terry, who is cruel, old-fashioned, and sardonic. The picture, a lurid melodrama, needs a few hatchet murders to enliven it. *The Caretakers,* and most of Crawford's subsequent thrillers, are generally looked upon as "high camp" by modern-day audiences, who juxtapose her aggressive, nasty roles with the tales (some feel *tall* tales) of child abuse told by her disinherited daughter Christina in her book, *Mommie Dearest.*

There were, however, plenty of hatchet murders in evidence in Crawford's next feature, *Strait-Jacket* (1964), which was directed by *Homicidal's* William Castle and written by *Psycho* novelist Robert Bloch. This picture is covered in Chapter Ten.

Crawford's next feature was *I Saw What You Did* (1965), another William Castle thriller, this one about two young women who get into trouble with a murderer they inadvertently contact during a childish phone game. This attempt more directly imitates *Psycho*, since its "best" sequence is an actual shower murder, though the victim is clothed and the scene is handled quite differently (and much less powerfully) than Hitchcock's classic terror scene. Joan Crawford and John Ireland are completely wasted. He is the murderer who butchers his drugged wife (Joyce Meadows) in the shower (to minimize spattering bloodstains), and Crawford is the amorous next door neighbor who realizes what he has done and gets stabbed in the belly for her trouble. Crawford is on screen for perhaps fifteen minutes in total.

Crawford's next shocker, though superior to *I Saw What You Did,* is another one that sounds a lot better than it plays. *Berserk* is a 1967 British chiller starring Crawford as Monica Rivers, the owner and ringmaster of a traveling Big Top who finds her box office zooming when some of the performers are brutally murdered. With accomplished treatment *Berserk* might have amounted to something—director Jim O'Connolly has never managed to rise above hack level—but there are a few reasonably effective scenes, including a murder sequence with a hammer and rivet, and a funny scene when a huge shadow chasing Crawford past the circus trailers turns out to belong to a friendly midget.

The less said about Crawford's final picture, *Trog* (1970)—another nominal horror item in which Crawford co-stars with a revivified prehistoric man—the better.

Although the aforementioned pictures, and the ones still to be discussed, kept these older ladies employed and introduced them to a whole new generation of fans, not everyone was enamored of these movies or what they did to their stars. Film historian Lawrence J. Quirk, author of books on such actresses as Joan Crawford and Claudette Colbert, says, "I remember the Bette Davis I grew up with, the effect she had on the millions of people across the country who loved her so much, her performances in sensitive, touching dramas like *The Old Maid*. And Joan Crawford giving truly fine performances in movies like *Possessed* and *Humoresque*. To see these once-great actresses belting each other and whacking people with axes fills me with sadness and regret."

In spite of understandable sentiments such as these from long-time admirers, other "aging actresses" rushed to appear in mostly tepid horror/suspense items. Barbara Stanwyck went the route with William Castle in *The Night Walker* (1964), the story of a woman haunted by recurring dreams involving her late husband. Stanwyck and ex-husband Robert Taylor were almost as bad as the script and Castle's usual insufficient direction.

Barbara Stanwyck confronts the dummy who wrote the script for *The Night Walker*.

On the set of *Lady in a Cage* with Olivia de Havilland (left) and Ann Southern.

Olivia de Havilland and Ann Sothern appeared in *Lady in a Cage* (1964), an imaginative, well-directed, and thought-provoking (if uneven and unpleasant) thriller about a wealthy woman who is menaced by psychopaths after she gets trapped in a private elevator. Walter Grauman directed. Not to be outdone by her sister (the two have been feuding for years), Joan Fontaine appeared in *The Devil's Own* (1967), a totally unneccessary story of a witches' coven ensnaring a hapless school teacher.

Shelley Winters appeared in a whole series of horror films, some of which are among the cinema's most lamentable products. The first was *The Mad Room* (1969), a remake of *Ladies in Retirement* tailored to fit in with the then current psycho-shocker obsession. The film is atmospheric and has interesting ingredients—a dotty old widow (Winters); two kids just released from a mental institution; and their psychotic older sister (Stella Stevens)—but, under Bernard Girard's uninspired direction, the picture is a big disappointment.

In 1971 Winters appeared in two films for director Curtis Harrington. The first was *What's the Matter With Helen?*, co-starring Debbie Reynolds. If the film has obvious similarities to *Baby Jane* it is probably because it, too, was written by Henry Farrell. Reynolds and Winters, the distraught mothers of two teen-aged murderers, begin life anew by opening a talent school for young girls in Hollywood in the 1930s. The macabre doings start to unfold when the ladies receive death threats. Winters, who is already unhinged by the events of the past,

In this scene from *The Devil's Own*, Joan Fontaine seems to be wondering, "What can I do next to top my sister, Olivia?"

loses her grip on reality and goes on a bloody rampage. Despite some nice touches and gruesome moments, the picture is entertaining but ridiculous.

But *Helen* is a masterpiece compared to *Who Slew Auntie Roo?*, a Hansel and Gretel take-off in which Winters, again cast as a batty widow, invites orphans for a Christmas get-together and decides to lock a couple of them up for safe-keeping. Again, there are suspenseful, stylish touches, but the bizarre events are more humorous than frightening. Winters' shrill phone-it-in performance is perhaps one of the ten or twenty worst of all time.

Winters, Bette Davis (in her later films), and other "aging" performers, particularly in films they have obvious contempt for, become grotesque, overblown caricatures of themselves. They don't seem to realize that, by deliberately giving unconvincing performances in films that they feel are not worthy of their talents, they not only make the films even worse than they already are but make themselves look like idiots in the bargain. Although Joan Crawford wasn't always at her peak in minor roles—her phone conversations to her married lover in *The Best of Everything*, for instance, were on the proficiency level of a high-school drama student—her otherwise professional attitude led one reviewer (of *Strait-Jacket*) to say "even in drek like this she gives a performance." Genuinely talented actresses can handle the wild, often improbable plots, the gory murders, and bizarre characterizations with little or no loss of dignity. Their less talented peers only reveal basic weaknesses that existed throughout their long careers but may not have been previously apparent.

Whatever Happened to Aunt Alice? (1969) was that fine actress Geraldine Page's entry into the genre. Page and co-star Ruth Gordon are far superior to their material, a good story ruined by Lee H. Katzin's routine direction. (This in spite of the fact that *Alice* was produced by *Baby Jane's* director, Robert Aldrich.) Page is superb as a psychotic widow who kills off all of her housemaids, receiving excellent support from Gordon as the feisty victim who decides she's not going to take things lying down.

Anxious to show how trendy they were and what good sports they could be—or just anxious for a part—other actresses lost no time in getting their chance to scream, faint, hack, and holler. Lauren Bacall radiated evil as a weird psychiatrist who goes nuts herself when her plans go awry in *Shock Treatment* (1964), a pretty bad melodrama, set in a mental institution, which is distinguished only by its opening scene: Roddy McDowall as a gardener using huge hedge clippers to snip off the head of his elderly employer (not shown graphically). Eleanor Parker fought off killer cats and the evil machinations of Gayle Hunnicutt in *Eye of the Cat* (1969). And Gloria Grahame played the nutty headmistress of an orphanage who freezes dead bodies in the inexplicable hope of bringing them

Geraldine Page shows brochures (for cemetery plots, no doubt) to her prospective victim, Ruth Gordon (right), in *Whatever Happened to Aunt Alice?*

back to life in the future in *Blood and Lace* (1971), a fairly energetic mix of grisliness and sadism that has a bizarre plot and some clever twists.

Patricia Neal did her duty in *The Night Digger* (1971), an evocative, better-than-average psychological thriller that details what happens when a disturbed young handyman enters the lives of two lonely women. Bernard Herrmann graced the film with a fine score, but Alastair Reid's direction substitutes style for sensitivity. Neal also appeared with Cloris Leachman in *Happy Mother's Day, Love George* (1973, a.k.a *Run, Stranger, Run*), a pretty good chiller directed by Darren McGavin. Tessa Dahl is excellent as the resident butcheress-at-large, and the late Bobby Darin is superb in a supporting role.

Besides appearing in *Hush . . . Hush, Sweet Charlotte* and *What's the Matter With Helen?*, Agnes Moorehead starred in a lively axe-murder movie entitled *Dear*

In spite of the grisly goings-on in *Cult of the Damned*, Jennifer Jones' mind seems to be elsewhere, (probably thinking of getting another agent).

Dead Delilah (1972). She plays a feisty dowager holding court over an old mansion full of the obligatory greedy relatives. While the film, directed by John Farris, has that almost inevitably choppy, low-budget crudeness about it, it also has many clever and imaginative touches. Practically the entire cast is killed off during the film's brief running time, and there's a zesty scene when a young lady in a wheelchair is decapitated by an assailant rushing past her on horseback. The picture is bloodily delightful, and Moorehead as good as ever. It's amusing to note that when TV stations run *Dear Dead Delilah* they usually cut the gory (but not terribly graphic) murders, yet those very same murders are reshown in smaller frames during the closing credits, which are never excised.

Even the inimitable Tallulah Bankhead made a horror flick, the entertaining *Die, Die, My Darling* (1965). The story of a religious fanatic (Bankhead) who imprisons her dead son's ex-fiancée in an effort to purify her, is even more timely in these Moral Majority days. Bankhead is campy but fun, while Stephanie

Powers as her victim, though appealing, gives a perfunctory performance. Donald Sutherland has a small role as the mental defective he was constantly playing early on in his career. Director Silvio Narizzano handles some scenes quite nicely, but as a whole the movie is sadistically interesting without being especially scary or effective.

Viveca Lindfors made a number of horror films during this period, including *A Cauldron of Blood* (with Boris Karloff) and the incomprehensible *A Bell from Hell*; she is still making them today, with *Creepshow* and *Silent Madness* among her

Ida Lupino beckons one and all to come bathe in *The Devil's Rain.*

Viveca Lindfors prepares a suspicious cup of tea for ailing Boris Karloff in 1970's *Cauldron of Blood*.

credits. Jennifer Jones appeared in a nominal horror item, *Cult of the Damned* (1970, a.k.a. *Angel, Angel, Down We Go*) presiding over a group of animalistic whackoes. Ida Lupino melted along with the rest of the cast when exposed to *The Devil's Rain* (1975), and the evil Martha Hyer was up to her armpits in nasty business in *Picture Mommy Dead* (1966).

Why did these women, some of whom had appeared in classic films, works of taste and refinement, bother to make these grisly ghoulies? Some, like Veronica Lake in *Flesh Feast* (1970), needed the money. Others, like Jones and Crawford, wanted to keep busy, and would appear in any dubious vehicle that might help keep their names before the public.

There were other terror trends in the sixties and seventies, including the horror anthology film, most of which were British movies following the tradition of the classic *Dead of Night* (1946). These films all feature four or five short horror tales loosely tied together by some plot strand, say five travelers on the same train, or four people told their fortunes by the same sneering gypsy; sometimes there is a final twist at the end which leads into the last, often humorous sequence. Typical entries include *Dr. Terror's House of Horrors* (1965) *Torture Garden* (1968), and *The Uncanny* (1977). Many of these pictures include segments that fit into the mad slasher/psycho-on-the-loose mold.

In 1972, stories from the old EC comic book, *Tales from the Crypt*, were adapted into an anthology film, which was followed by an adaptation of *Crypt*'s companion mag, *Vault of Horror*. Joan Collins appears in *Tales from the Crypt* and

Joan Collins was co-starring with killer treetrunks in movies like *Tales that Witness Madness* in the seventies. No wonder she signed up with *Dynasty*.

Tales that Witness Madness (1973), and in fact made so many horror films (*The Devil Within Her, Inn of the Frightened People*) in the sixties and seventies that she came close to being crowned queen of horror before being rescued by producer Aaron Spelling to play the bitchy Alexis Carrington Colby Dexter on the superficial night-time soaper, *Dynasty.*

In *Tales that Witness Madness,* directed by the prolific but pedestrian Freddie Francis, who also did *Crypt,* Collins appears in a funny episode about a battle between a wife and a vicious tree-trunk—yes, tree trunk—that has unnatural designs on her husband. (Could a tree trunk's designs be anything but unnatural?) Kim Novak also appears in a gruesome sequence in *Madness* in which her daughter winds up as the main course at a luau.

The problem with many of these anthology films is that there isn't enough imagination on tap for one story, let alone five, and many of the segments come off as tired *Twilight Zone* rejects. Robert Bloch wrote the script for at least two of these offerings, *The House that Dripped Blood* (1971) and *Asylum* (1972), but surely didn't strain himself coming up with the tepid ideas for either film, the first of which is a quartet of disappointing stories tied around an old English manor. The most interesting of the four is a tale about a writer who swears that he can see a homicidal character he created walking around the grounds, but this and the other three stories are either out and out parodies or fail to completely develop their intriguing premises. Peter Duffell's inept direction does little to bolster the proceedings.

In *Asylum,* directed by Roy Ward Baker, Bloch came up with a clever scene when the pieces of a dismembered body—covered up with brown wrapping paper—come to life to wreak bloody havoc, but the sequence is too laughably executed to be effective; another segment, featuring the umpteenth homicidal split-personality story, is so obvious it's pointless. The bridge between stories is that the main character in each segment is a resident in a sinister mental hospital.

Horror anthologies have found a fairly welcoming home on television, but cinema equivalents show up infrequently. *Nightmares* (1984), which was originally made for television, and the Stephen King/George Romero collaboration on *Creepshow* are two of the most recent. For many of us, horror works best full-length, when it has time to come to a full bloody boil.

There were a number of other interesting shockers made during this period, many of them indirectly influenced by *Psycho.* Stories about split personalities and people with odd sexual histories who become psychotic were in abundance. In *The Name of the Game is Kill* (a.k.a. *The Female Trap*/1968), Jack Lord plays a drifter who gets involved with a nutty family of three disturbed daughters (including Susan Strasberg) and their alleged mother (female impersonator

T.C. Jones). The impossible premise is that the father spent years dressing up as and pretending to be his late wife in order to protect the daughter who killed her. In spite of the fact that the audience can see through the deception from the first, the man's own children are unable to penetrate his disguise! At one point in the movie someone gets bludgeoned with a Venus de Milo statue. Susan Strasberg's performance helps add to an atmosphere of desperation and loneliness; otherwise Gunnar Hellstrom's film is utterly forgettable.

From across the ocean came a variety of gruesome British films in the best Grand Guignol tradition, including *Theater of Death* (1967), in which the members of a Parisian drama troupe are involved in a series of bizarre slayings. It's stylish and atmospheric, but unspectacular. *Psycho-Circus* (1967/a.k.a *Circus of Fear*) is about a murderer stalking the big top. Christoper Lee appears in both these films, and many other similar, often interchangeable, items.

Peter Cushing took time off from his usual vampire movies to appear in *Corruption*, a wild, lurid 1968 thriller in which he plays a surgeon who attempts to fix a girlfriend's disfigured face by using the pituitary glands of women he kills and then decapitates. This gamey, gruesome film is almost ruined by Robert Hartford-Davis' pedestrian direction and a terribly inappropriate jazz score, but has some effective scenes, including a murder on a train and a remarkable finale when a laser tool goes berserk and kills virtually the entire cast in one fell swoop.

The Twisted Nerve (1968), graced with another Bernard Herrmann score, is about a disturbed young man with multiple personalities and a penchant for threatening women with hatchets. (For the controversial aspects of this chiller, see Chapter Five.)

Meanwhile, on American shores, Anthony Perkins resurfaced in another well-received but overrated thriller, *Pretty Poison* (1968), playing a disturbed young man who meets up with a sociopathic young lady (Tuesday Weld) in a small town. Of course this encounter leads to a series of murders. Noel Black's direction is good, but the picture lacks that certain finesse that would have made it really spine-tingling. Beverly Garland, a good actress whose career has been lost in dreadful Grade-D horror items and forgettable TV shows, offers the best performance in the film, as Weld's mother.

The early seventies were busy years for shockers. The lovable Vincent Price appeared in Robert Fuest's campy art deco horror films *The Abominable Dr. Phibes* (1971), and its sequel, *Dr. Phibes Rises Again* (1972). In the first film, Dr. Phibes (Price) kills off the doctors he believes are responsible for his wife's death by recreating ancient Biblical plagues. In the second, he takes out his aggressions on a group of nosy archeologists who are digging too close to his tomb. The sets are superb, Fuest's direction stylish, but how much you enjoy the *Phibes* films depends on your tolerance for this particular subgenre, an uneasy but often

The Twisted Nerve: "A penchant for threatening women with hatchets."

hilarious blend of perverse chuckles and fiendish bloodshed. Some might find the display of death after death to be comparatively boring and singularly unchilling, though both movies have a fair amount of suspense, and their gruesome moments were good indications of the graphic carnality that was to overtake the horror film in the years to come.

Price did at least one other film in a similar vein, Douglas Hickox' *Theater of Blood* (1973), in which ham actor Price performs murders a la Shakespeare. His victims are those critics who neglected to properly honor his performances. A witty, if tasteless, mixture of laughs and gore, it was well-received by real critics, most of whom lamented the graphic bloodshed (tame by today's standards), which includes heads sawed off sleeping victims and left outside doors, and the like. *Theater of Blood* is no masterpiece, but it has a sort of oddball, novel charm.

Two of the most interesting items of 1971 were *Hands of the Ripper* and *Play Misty for Me*. *Ripper* is perhaps the best work of the uneven but promising British director Peter Sasdy. It concerns the daughter of Jack the Ripper, who has been psychotic since babyhood, when she saw Dad murder her mother at cribside. A misguided psychiatrist tries to help her, but she suffers frequent homicidal blackouts, during which she is unable to stop murdering women. The film, though far from perfect, is lively, atmospheric, and fairly energetic.

Misty was directed by Clint Eastwood, of all people, who also stars in this story of a disc jockey whose life is made a shambles by a psychotic fan (a vivid Jessica Walter) who calls him up with the request, "Play *Misty* for me." She sleeps with him and tries to run his life, while he tries unsuccessfully to ditch her for the more stable Donna Mills. The film received excellent notices; of particular interest was the bloody sequence when the deranged Walter attacks Eastwood's maid with a butcher knife. This sequence, which boasts tight, impressive, *Psycho*-like editing, had critics comparing Eastwood to Hitchcock and predicting great things on the horizon for the actor-turned-director. (None of which have materialized; Eastwood's other efforts, both as star and director, have been fairly mediocre.) *Misty* has flaccid moments, including a long, unnecessary sequence with Eastwood and Mills strolling to a Roberta Flack melody, but is otherwise one of the best thrillers of the period.

When *Misty* was re-released as the bottom half of a double bill with Alfred Hitchcock's *Frenzy* the following year, many people thought Eastwood's film was better—or at least more entertaining—than the master's. But aside from the aforementioned stabbing scene (usually cut for television) and a pretty tense finale, *Misty* doesn't hold up quite as well as *Frenzy* does, at least not to the more discerning.

1971 also saw the release of Richard Fleischer's *See No Evil* about a blind girl (Mia Farrow) being stalked by a murderer who has slaughtered her entire family. This lukewarm film tries to do for the bathtub what *Psycho* did for the shower (someone is brutally strangled while doing the rub-a-dub-dub bit), but the scene is so dismally handled that it won't discourage anyone from taking a bath.

Shockers of 1972 run the gamut from absorbing to abysmal. Forgettable items include Edward Dmytryk's *Bluebeard*, with Richard Burton giving another wretched performance as a mass murderer of beautiful women; *Crescendo*, a very silly, trite, and predictable psycho-suspense film with Stephanie Powers involved with the usual loonies, including James Olsen as "twin" brothers; and Peter Collinson's *Straight on Till Morning*, a very strange picture with Rita Tushingham. She plays a lonely, troubled woman who agrees to do the cooking and cleaning for a handsome blond—who turns out to a psycho, of course—providing he agrees to give her a baby. The innovative editing, which completely disregards chronology, is too frenetic, and the picture doesn't really work. However, Shane Briant, as the psycho, is given a terrific monologue to explain his "abuse" at the hands of the older women he murders.

Somewhat better are *The Night Visitor*, with Max Von Sydow periodically escaping from the asylum he is incarcerated in to use his axe on Liv Ullmann and others who helped to unjustly imprison him, and *The Possession of Joel Delaney*, in which Shirley MacLaine discovers that her handsome brother (Perry King) has been possessed by a dead man who had a habit of decapitating women. The film has a striking textural quality, effective atmosphere, and excellent New York City location filming, but director Waris Hussein fails to construct it as a solid thriller.

Two notable, and very different, 1972 efforts are the film version of Tom Tryon's novel, *The Other*, and the bizarre low-budget *The Folks at Redwolf Inn* (a.k.a. *Terror House*). *The Other* is another story about twins, this time young boys, one of whom has passed away before the story begins. The one who is alive has a split personality and raises all kinds of havoc, which he blames on his poor dead brother. While *The Other*, under director Robert Mulligan's guidance, is not perfect by any means, the obvious developments of its plot and its pedestrian moments are overshadowed by the sheer tragic poignancy of the story. Many scenes have undeniable power: young Miles' journey into the mind of a flying crow; the death of his father; and the awful climactic scene with the missing baby in the barrel. Despite its flaws, *The Other* remains a fine exercise in the macabre and is a very sad picture indeed.

The Folks at Redwolf Inn is a sick comedy-horror flick about an elderly couple who run an isolated lodge and put their nubile guests on the menu. Those who can stomach the gross goings-on will find this a rather darkly amusing and disturbing little chiller, well directed by Bud Townsend. It's an imaginative picture, with a grotesque and funny finale.

There were three interesting items in 1973. *Wicked, Wicked* is a fairly lousy but entertaining psycho-on-the-loose-in-a-large-hotel story, distinguished only in that the *entire* film is shown in splitscreen "duo vision." *Silent Night, Bloody Night* is an uneven but atmospheric chiller with a splendid premise—virtually all the residents of a town are actually asylum inmates who broke out of the institution and slaughtered their doctors years ago in one bloody night. The main selling point for this film was a scene in which Patrick O'Neal and Astrid Heeren are cornered in the bedroom by an axe-wielding assailant. The scene, which doesn't compare favorably to the *Psycho* shower murder, consists of shots of a swinging axe spliced together with reaction head shots of the two victims, with much blood spattered on the walls and everywhere else. It's a perfect example of how technical proficiency and editing were beginning to be replaced by mere "splatter" in the early seventies. *Silent Night* was directed by Theodore Gershuny. *Reflection of Fear* is another fairly direct *Psycho* imitation about a disturbed young woman (Sondra Locke) who lives with her mother and grandma and a mysterious unseen companion named Aaron. Trouble brews when her father (Robert Shaw) and his girlfriend (Sally Kellerman) reappear on the scene after a lengthy absence, and Mom and Grandma are strangled and bludgeoned to death respectively. This obvious thriller has one decent murder sequence and some atmosphere, but it's readily apparent that young Marguerite (Locke) is dressing up as "Aaron" and doing the dirty work. To make matters worse, we discover that poor Marguerite was born a *boy*, and was forced to play the role of daughter at maternal insistence (the opposite of the plot twist used in *Homicidal*). This gimmick of a boy disguised and being raised as a girl resurfaced later in the 1983 thriller, *Sleepaway Camp*, and carried much more of a wallop.

Psychic Killer (1975) cashed in on the public's fascination with ESP, mental telepathy, and such, but this revenge story of Jim Hutton picking off victims one by one with the power of his mind has only one interesting scene, a gruesome one of a butcher (Neville Brand) getting the same treatment as his prime cutlets. *Deadly Strangers* (1975) features Hayley Mills as a hitchhiker, Simon Ward as the man who picks her up, and a town they pass through where a lunatic has (conveniently) just escaped from the local asylum. The film is distinguished by a completely unexpected final twist.

Although many of the horror films of this period were junky, derivative, and idiotic, there was the occasional item of genuine quality. One fine example is Larry Yust's ingenious *Homebodies* (1974). The film is a very good, rather grotesque horror film with comedy/drama overtones about elderly people who strike back with a vengeance at the officials who want to evict them. At the same time, horrible accidents are plaguing the workers building a huge high-rise that will tower over the neighborhood. *Homebodies* is a perfect example of how a talented, imaginative director can work within a very low budget and come up with something clever and pictorially interesting. Kudos go to the cast, also— both the marvelous senior citizens and their younger, supporting players.

Inspired by the success of Dario Argento's early thrillers, distributors began to release dubbed versions of foreign-language shockers from various countries, some of which were far bloodier than the American product of the same period. Argento and some of his peers had an undeniable influence on American horror filmmakers, who were still using blood with some restraint. Independent features that played 42nd Street and its counterparts, as well as drive-ins and local theaters during all-night horror marathons, were more on a par with foreign releases, so far as bloodletting was concerned. These films got away with much more nastiness, grossness, and graphic mayhem than the films already discussed in this chapter, and helped bring about a new era of gore in the mainstream terror pictures of the period to follow.

From Italy we got films by Argento imitators such as Sergio Martino (*Next*/ 1970—a mad killer slashes women with a straight-razor in Vienna); Armando Crispino (*The Dead Are Alive*/1972—a fruitcake bludgeons necking couples

She-Devils on Wheels, one of Herschell Gordon Lewis' gory independents. Note the phony severed head in the foreground.

around an archeological dig to the strains of grand opera); and Emilio Miraglia (*The Night Evelyn Came Out of the Grave*/1971, featuring a truly vomitous scene of an old woman getting torn apart by wolves.) All of these films, though flawed, contain bizarre characters and stylish touches in the lushest Italian manner, not to mention an alarming passion for violence and mutilation. The imagery in these Italian thrillers is often striking. In *Spasmo* there is a forest full of life-size mannequins; these same dummies show up later in a torture chamber where a weird masked man ties up and abuses women. (Perhaps those same dummies were responsible for *Spasmo*'s screenplay.)

Gruesome Mexican films were in abundance, and Spain sent over *The House That Screamed* in 1970, a tale of a murderer in a girls' school. This film also qualifies as an "aging actress" picture in that Lilli Palmer dubs her own voice as the stern, sadistic headmistress. Directed by Narciso Ibanez Serrador, *The House*

That Screamed isn't half-bad, in spite of the usual imperfections and lapses. Even Germany got into the act with the marvelously titled *Torture Chamber of Dr. Sadism* (1967), a surprisingly tame rip-off of Poe's *Pit and the Pendulum* starring Lex Barker and Christopher Lee.

Meanwhile, many Americans who found themselves with an inheritance and nothing to spend it on decided to try turning a tidy profit by making a low-budget exploitation film. Horror films seemed the easiest—and legally safest—to attempt. Most of these films don't exhibit the kind of stylish, imaginative treatment that might have lifted them above the scrap heap. Even those that do have a few promising moments are so technically insufficient and amateurish, production-wise, that it is a wonder they were ever released. The only thing some of these films have going for them is gore. Even on that level the films are pretty cheap and unconvincing. Some took a page from George Romero's book and used real animal offal as a stand in for gouged-out human guts. (These films' victims have a tendency to lose their "innards" even from the flimsiest wounds—and audiences have a tendency to lose their lunches!) With or without animal offal, some of these films are too laughable to take seriously.

Invasion of the Blood Farmers, Torture Dungeon, Don't Look in the Basement, Children Shouldn't Play With Dead Things, House of Seven Corpses, So Sad About Gloria, My Brother Has Bad Dreams, Decoy for Terror, Warlock Moon—it's hard to say which of these and so many others is worse. But perhaps that distinction goes, collectively, to the abysmal films of Herschell Gordon Lewis, who directed several ultra-gory (and ultra-phony) horror films of the sixties (with titles like *She Devils on Wheels*) about which no one has ever said anything nice. Lewis is often referred to as the Grandfather of Gore, the Father of Modern-Day Splatter Movies, and so on, because he was the first director to resort to using what had to be socially objectionable acts of violence in his movies; a dubious achievement indeed. Reportedly his movies are worthless on virtually every level—and this from the man's *admirers*.

Besides being terrible filmmakers, Lewis and others of his ilk are utterly passé today. Major studios took over the distribution of gory low-budget movies in the late seventies. They spent millions of dollars making high-gloss, mainstream horror movies that outclassed the grisly independent cheapies with state-of-the-art makeup effects and streamlined production values, beating them at their own game.

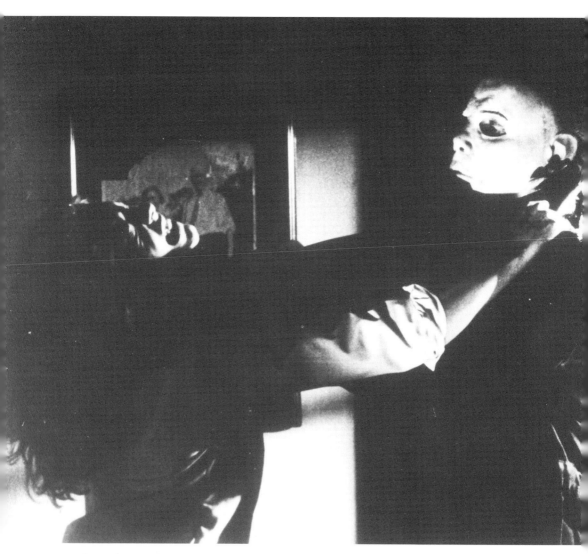

Maniac "Michael Myers" strangles a squirming victim in John Carpenter's over-rated *Halloween*.

STALK AND SLASH

A tidal wave of a particular type of horror film, the "stalk-and-slash" movie, which refers to the antisocial habits of the psychopaths who inhabit these films, was unleashed in 1978 when John Carpenter's film, *Halloween*, came to the screen. The movie cost very little to make, but grossed millions as long lines formed at the box office. Although Carpenter had made other low-budget films before *Halloween*, this suspense shocker was the one that put him on the map.

The question is, why? The simple truth of the matter is that *Halloween* is not a terribly good picture. It has a nice premise: a little boy who stabbed his sister to death escapes from an institution on Halloween many years later and returns to the scene of the crime. It has the usual victims: nubile schoolgirls, barking dogs, and at least one amorous boyfriend. The trappings are all there for an exceptional horror film: atmospheric photography and music, good locations. For the most part, however, *Halloween* is a lackluster, frequently tedious movie that misses virtually every possibility for further development in terms of character, story line, and even suspense. Carpenter's own musical score is so repetitive that whatever effectiveness it might have is gradually dissipated. Worse yet, the movie rips off the far superior (but less polished) *Texas Chainsaw Massacre* by using a killer who wears a mask over his face.

Bloodless and pedestrian, *Halloween* just sits there when it should be doing something. Of course, there have been so many similar items since it first appeared that subsequent viewings have the built-in handicap of over-familiarity. In spite of this, anyone who looks at *Halloween* objectively will see that, while it is clearly superior to much of the competition, and director Carpenter shows promise, it is not nearly as good as some critics would have us believe.

Why, then, was it so successful? A lot of credit must go to an ad campaign that printed verbatim a review that made it sound as if *Halloween* were the greatest thing since *Psycho*, and Carpenter the newest Hitchcock. (Film reviewers who want to attract attention know that the easiest way to do that is to write an unqualified rave for a lousy picture. Publicity departments aren't able to resist quoting it.) While it is true that horror films are critic-proof in the sense that a bad review won't discourage hardcore fans from seeing a particular picture (especially when they consider that few critics are fond of horror movies) a positive review is so unusual that it serves to attract a very large crossover audience, including people who might normally avoid "mad slasher" movies at all costs. *Halloween*'s comparative tastefulness, good reviews, and low budget made it a sure-fire winner at the box office.

Halloween had a tremendous effect on the career of its young star, Jamie Lee Curtis (the daughter of Janet Leigh and Tony Curtis). After *Halloween*'s success the actress found herself cast in a series of similar pictures and was well on her way to becoming a 1980's "queen of horror" before she jumped ship and landed roles in more "serious" vehicles (such as *Trading Places* and *Grandview U.S.A.*). She appeared in *Prom Night* (1980), which is a pretty dismal blend of *Carrie*, *Halloween*, and, of all things, *Saturday Night Fever*. A killer stalks wenches and their dates at the title fête. As well, Curtis was in *Terror Train* (1980), in which a youth gets revenge on the "friends" who'd once played a nasty trick on him (they manuevered him into bed with a dismembered corpse) by stalking and killing them on an excursion train sponsored by a fraternity brother. It is forgettable but for a few grisly passages.

Curtis also appeared in *The Fog* (1980), Carpenter's next film, a creditable supernatural tale about lepers who rise from the grave to get revenge on the descendants of the town's founding fathers, who had sunk the lepers' ship rather than allow the afflicted people to live among them.

Meanwhile, the story that was told in *Halloween* wasn't quite over. (With grosses like that, there had to be a sequel.) By this time, the phenomenally popular *Friday the 13th* had opened and broken box office records, spawning its own imitations and rip-offs. Although Carpenter's film was not especially tasteless or graphic, the powers-that-be knew that its sequel would have to be on the bloodletting level of *Friday* if it were to tower over the very competition it had brought into being.

Halloween Two (1981) was directed by Rick Rosenthal (Carpenter produced, and wrote the screenplay with Debra Hill), and begins where the first picture ends. Jamie Lee, who has survived the maniac's attack in *Halloween*, has been taken to the hospital. "Michael Myers," the maniac, cuts a bloody swath on his way to finish what he started: slicing up Jamie Lee. (It turns out that Curtis was adopted and is actually the maniac's *other* sister.) At the hospital Myers eliminates virtually the entire staff. He drowns them in whirlpool baths, stabs them with

"Michael Myers" sneaks up on another victim in *Halloween Two*.

knives and needles and dispatches one poor fellow with a hammer in the head. Clearly *Halloween Two* was influenced more by the stalk-and-slash films that followed in *Halloween's* wake than by the original.

Donald Pleasance (a good actor giving a terrible, hammy performance) repeats his role as Michael's psychiatrist, who seems convinced that Myers is the boogey man, a miniature Antichrist or "God of Death," and his almost supernatural ability to survive bullets, fires, and explosions would seem to bear this out. *Halloween Two*, while almost as slow-moving as Carpenter's film, is nonetheless more entertaining than *Halloween*, if only because the body count is higher and the murders more flamboyant.

In *Halloween Three: Season of the Witch* (1982), there is no sign of Michael Myers, Jamie Lee Curtis, or Donald Pleasance. *Halloween Three* is actually an imaginative suspense story that blends witchcraft and technology in a diabolical plot to kill off most of the country's children, and their parents, on Allhallows eve (via diabolical novelty masks). Far more than a mere stalk-and-slash film, *Halloween Three* is much more interesting and riveting than parts one and two put together. Instead of simply detailing (and telegraphing) one unsurprising murder after another, *Halloween Three* sets up a conflict of epic proportions between a pleasant young couple and a loathesome antagonist who will bring about the deaths of thousands of people (not just a few teenagers) if he's not stopped in time. The most shocking, indeed, depressing, aspect of the picture is that the villain's plot succeeds!

Oddly enough, *Halloween Three* contains much more graphic violence than the first two films. A man's skull is crushed; another man's head is literally ripped off his body; a woman's face is horribly disfigured by a laser beam. Most stalk-and-slash films are so devoid of interesting elements that they require scenes of an explicitly gruesome nature. Since *Halloween Three*'s story line exhibits much more inventiveness than usual, its gory scenes almost seem gratuitous. Writer/director Tommy Lee Wallace moves things at too slow a pace, but otherwise the film is quite entertaining and original. Dan O'Herlihy seems to be enjoying himself as the villainous mastermind.

If *Halloween* was the cinema's first horror trilogy, *Friday the 13th* became the first horror *quintet*! To date there have been five installments in the series: the fourth, subtitled *The Final Chapter*, was followed by the fifth, sub-titled *A New Beginning*.

Friday the 13th (1980) is the ultimate stalk-and-slash movie. A summer camp that was the scene of a double murder many years before is reopened, but while the counselors fix up the place and prepare for the onslaught of kiddies, they are gruesomely (and rapidly) dispatched by an unseen killer fond of knives, axes, and the like. Talentwise, director Sean Cunningham is not even on the level of John Carpenter, but the picture has a certain fiendish energy, and is frightening and suspenseful in a perverse, cheapjack manner. The basic premise is so grotesque—an idyllic camp setting transformed into a charnel house—that even slow, badly directed scenes (and there are many) hold the attention of the audience. The on-location filming adds immeasurably to the film's grim, relentless atmosphere. Harry Manfredini's derivative music for this and the sequels—he imitates everything from *Psycho* to *Jaws*—is serviceable, but the "ch-ch-ch" sounds and "pow-pow-pow" verbalizations on the soundtrack are a bit much. There are enough grisly shocks and surprises to satisfy the most jaded, bloodthirsty customer.

Adrienne King comes upon another hacked-up victim of the killer in the atmospheric *Friday the 13th.*

Of course the best element in the film is the identity of the killer, the sinister Mrs. Vorhees (Betsy Palmer). The deranged woman (the former cook of Camp Crystal Lake) lost her retarded son Jason because two camp counselors many years ago had been making love when they should have been watching him as he took a dip in the lake. (Palmer later killed them.) "I—I couldn't let them open the camp again, c—could I?" she asks her last victim-to-be, the plucky Adrienne King. Seeing the formerly innocuous Ms. Palmer engaging in the horrendous acts she's called upon to do in the script is surely a most delicious illustration of incongruity. Palmer is wonderfully sinister, both frightening and amusing at the same time. Some of *Friday*'s best moments, including the eerie flashbacks to Jason's drowning, occur when she's on screen. The climax of the picture has King turning on her pursuer and decapitating Palmer with a machete.

Jason Vorhees' shrine to his mother (at least her head) in *Friday the 13th Part Two* is a charnel house of dead bodies and skeletons.

Steve Miner replaced Cunningham for *Friday the 13th Part Two* (1981), but he wasn't much of an improvement when it came to style and craftsmanship. In Part Two it turns out that Jason didn't drown in the lake after all (why his mother, who killed the counselors for revenge over her son's *death*, didn't know he was alive has never been explained), but has been living in the woods all these years. Now he wants to get even for his mother's decapitation. (He keeps her head as a sort of shrine in the shack he lives in.) Young men and women at a counselor-training camp across the lake from "Camp Blood" (the rechristened Camp Crystal Lake) are slaughtered by the grown-up Jason, who wears a sack over his head to hide his hideously disfigured face. The picture is basically an entertaining reworking of *Friday Part One*.

Part Two was followed up with *Friday the 13th Part Three in 3D* (1982), in which Jason, still alive, kills off anyone he comes into contact with as his territorial

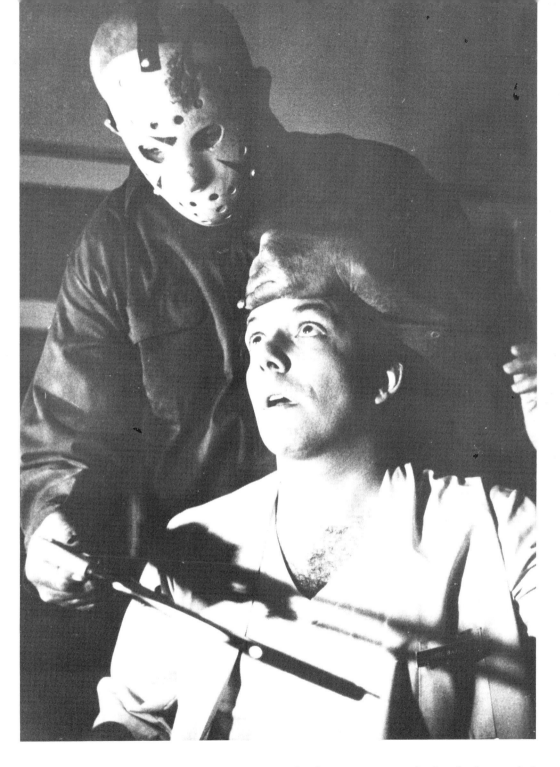

The diabolical Jason Vorhees is about to use a hacksaw to remove the head of a startled victim in *Friday the 13th—The Final Chapter*.

imperative dictates. In this case, a young lady and her friends spending time on her parent's farm are his latest victims. As impervious to death and injury as Michael Myers, Jason survives a hatchet in the head to return in *Friday the 13th: The Final Chapter* (1984), in which he attacks a new group of vacationing teenagers. He's finally killed off, hacked to pieces by a young boy who's defending his older sister. Joseph Zito's direction in this fourth episode is so wretched that the old formula is completely devoid of entertainment value.

In *Friday the 13th Part Five: A New Beginning* (1985), Tommy, the young boy who killed Jason, is now a teen-ager readjusting to life in a home for emotionally disturbed youngsters. Apparently Jason has come back from the grave to commit a new series of murders (*seventeen* of them, in fact). Danny Steinman's direction is adequate for presenting the succession of stabs and slashes, but nothing more. There's an ingenious plot twist at the end—someone besides Jason (or Tommy) is behind the slaughter—but Steinman even gives that away too early with his unsubtle approach. At the end, the real killer has met his maker, but it's clear that young Tommy is finally ready to take over Jason's legacy. The first murder in *A New Beginning* is by far the most horrendous in the series, if only because it's totally unexpected. It takes place in broad daylight, and while not part of the general slaughter, actually precipitates it. Whatever the faults of the *Friday* series, there's no denying that Jason Vorhees has become a mythical and powerful figure in the annals of popular screen horror.

It's too bad that the producers of the series have such contempt for their audience. There are way too many plot holes and implausibilities. The pictures are fun but sick. Why couldn't the producers have insisted on screenplays that bothered to create three-dimensional characters and dealt with maniac Jason on a human, as well as monster, level? If there were some substance to the narratives, some interesting ingredients aside from the slaughter, the *Friday* series could have satisfied the less demanding fans with its violence and also provided discriminating horror-movie lovers with something not quite so mindless and moronic.

Additionally, the murder scenes in all five *Friday* pictures are handled in the same way. There is none of the skillful, tight, imaginative editing of *Psycho's* shower murder. The effectiveness of the *Friday* deaths all depend on the cleverness of the shock/surprise element and the "gross out" factor of the gory makeup tricks, which are pretty well done, if at times gratuitously tasteless.

After five films it has still not been explained why Jason simply didn't go home to Mommy after dragging himself out of the lake that fateful day. (And that's just one of the inconsistencies, one that is not likely to be cleared up now that Jason is dead.)

Also worthy of note is the cinema's third horror trilogy (discounting all the

A nosy reporter (Liz Shephard) is attacked by a crow sent by the anti-Christ to slay her in *Damien: Omen Two*, the rousing sequel to *The Omen*.

Frankenstein and *Dracula* series of the forties). The three of the *The Omen* series are large-scale, big-budget movies that exhibit far better production values than the tacky stalk-and-slashers already mentioned—*without* stinting on the gore. Taken together, the trilogy details the birth, life, and death of Damien Thorn, the Antichrist, born of a jackal and substituted for the child of ambassador Gregory Peck and his wife Lee Remick. The orphaned Damien is a teen-aged boy in *Damien: Omen Two* (with foster parents William Holden and Lee Grant), and a handsome grown man played by Sam Neill in *The Final Conflict*, the third and final picture in the series. While Damien tries to get a grip on various industrial and technological hierarchies in order to effect a demonic takeover of the world, anyone who gets in his way is impaled, decapitated, or thrown out of the building.

The original *Omen* (1976) is more atmospheric and suspenseful than its sequels, with richer characters and an eerier ambience. Director Richard Donner often needs a steadier hand, but many of the scenes are quite effective, including a nightmarish sequence in a cemetery crawling with vicious dogs, and Lee Remick's fantastic plunge out of a hospital window. *Damien: Omen Two* (1978) is more thrilling and technically polished in spots than *The Omen*, as if director Don Taylor were striving for a more epic approach than the darker, more personal aura of the original. He does a splendid job of reworking and outdoing *The Omen*'s already flamboyant death scenes. Liz Shephard's death—her eyes pecked out by a crow before she wanders into the path of a Mack truck—is particularly memorable.

The main problem with all three films in the series is the consistent and stubbornly unthoughtful approach. (Andrew Birkin's screenplay for *The Final Conflict* is the silliest of the lot.) Various plot elements go unexplained and unrealized, and the religious aspects of the story line cannot be taken seriously, even by the devoutly faithful. *The Omen* series is chilling, exciting—but utterly superficial. As horror movies, however, they beat out most of the competition. *The Final Conflict* (1981), under Graham Baker's slick direction, overcomes its foolish premise with some excellent sequences: a baby carriage careening down a slope; the death of Damien's private secretary (his wife gets him with her iron); a double murder on an old English bridge; and a body set on fire as it swings and dangles above a studio set.

Jerry Goldsmith's music for all three films is excellent. In *Damien: Omen Two* there is a particular richness and variety that embellishes every scene. As the *Village Voice* put it when reviewing *Damien: Omen Two*: "Producer Bernhard has maintained the standard of treating each killing as an eerily poetic coup de grace. And every massacre is accompanied by a prologue, death march, and coda provided by Oscar-winning Jerry Goldsmith's colloquial and ecstatic rendition of a blithe Dies Irae." In *The Omen*, the music that heralds ominous events or signifies silent communication between Damien and the devil's (sometimes non-human) minions is terrifying.

The *Omen* films had their share of imitations. *The Chosen* (1978), with the charismatic Kirk Douglas, is almost as much a sequel to *The Omen* as *Damien: Omen Two* is. This story of an industrialist and his demonic son packs a few grisly wallops. *The Awakening* (1980), a dreadful remake of the far superior *Blood from the Mummy's Tomb* (1972), substitutes a young woman possessed by the spirit of a mummified princess for the Antichrist; it is a perfect illustration of how *not* to make an epic thriller. Director Mike Newell's general ineptness at portraying the obligatory flamboyant deaths (in some cases the audience wasn't sure how, why, or *if* somebody had been killed!) proves that putting together slick, big-budget horror films and making them *work* (on any level) isn't as easy as it looks.

Meanwhile, the smaller studios were churning out more *Halloween* and *Friday the 13th* clones, with camps, small towns, college campuses, and even high schools as the settings for gruesome tales of maniacal mayhem. A few of these pictures exhibit a modicum of style and some imagination—at least in the violent death sequences—but most are just dreadful, far below even the level of the films that inspired them.

Stalk-and-slash items are made cheaply and filmed cheaply. Good actors (and a few, including unknowns, are better than the material) can do a lot to help put a picture over. Excellent makeup effects, or simply a speedy pace, can sufficiently aid a terrible script. Unfortunately, far too many of these movies crawl along at a snail's pace, feature terrible actors mouthing unutterable dialogue, and even on occasion employ mediocre makeup and special effects, which really adds insult to injury.

Hack directors have not learned that if they want to sustain suspense and tension, the worst thing they can do is to make pictures with too few camera set-ups, which result in flaccid editing. A picture has to *move*—shot after shot, viewpoint following viewpoint—and the pace should only slow down, the shot should only be held, if doing so serves a particular purpose. The audience must never have time to cough, fidget, or wonder about the believability of the proceedings. Sometimes there can be compensating elements in a badly made movie, something that keeps the audience's attention from wandering during scenes that plod along haphazardly without aim or guidance. But since all that the copy-cat stalk-and-slash films have to offer is the same old, tired formula, most are snooze-inducers instead of thrillers.

Too many of these pictures consist of long expository scenes—sometimes consisting of three-fourths or more of a picture's running time—which detail the boring lives and activities of dreary, uninteresting teen-agers before they each get murdered (as if in sacrifice to the restless audience). Endless discussions of joints, sex, and booze are interspersed with the occasional flash of a knife or a grisly beheading. No wonder the glut of stalk-and-slash films almost put an end to this sub-category of the genre.

We could blame the relative inexperience of some of the directors of these movies for their low quality level, except that even veteran directors turn in botched-up jobs. J. Lee Thompson is a case in point. His *Happy Birthday to Me* (1981), with Melissa Sue Anderson and Glenn Ford, is easily one of the worst pictures of the period.

There are some fairly lively, if mediocre, *Friday* imitations, such as *The Burning*, *Sleepaway Camp*, and *Madman*. The weakest of the three pictures, *The Burning* (1981), at least has one novel variation on the usual stalk-and-slash formula. The maniac, "Cropsy," a disfigured camp caretaker "getting even" with the coun-selors, just doesn't skulk around in the shadows at night attacking lone victims like Jason Vorhees. Jumping up from what the kids *think* is an abandoned canoe, he uses his gardening shears to slaughter *six of them at once* in broad daylight, hacking and hewing at their bodies before they have a chance to defend themselves.

Other movies about maniacs stalking coeds and their boyfriends include *The House on Sorority Row, Final Exam, Hell Night, The Co-Ed Murders, Graduation Day, The Dorm that Dripped Blood*, and, wouldn't you know it, *Splatter University*. Another one, *The Prowler* (1981), has a handsomely produced opening segment at a 1944 graduation dance (and a pitchfork murder) that suggests, for once, a real class item is unfolding. Alas, once we get to the contemporary segment that forms the rest of the picture, Joseph Zito's abysmal direction quickly jettisons that idea. *The Prowler* is typical of many films in the genre in that the motives of the killer (in this case a sheriff played by Farley Granger) are never even explained. This can be the distributor's fault (important plot elements are sometimes left on the cutting-room floor when they arbitrarily decide to trim a picture's running time), but more often it's strictly the fault of a weak screenplay, or direction and editing that fail to make clear exactly what is going on.

In most stalk-and-slash films the "mysterious" identity of the killer is so obvious that there is no tension whatsoever on that angle. Character motivations and psychological histories are dubious, to say the least. As well, anyone can be conveniently psychopathic—so as to twist the plot in any direction that seems to serve the gore-heavy demands of the story line.

Naturally, the gore in these splatter movies has become their *raison d'etre*. Makeup artists like Tom Savini (the top dog) and Carl Fullerton are becoming mini-celebrities. Ironically, some of their shocking, meticulous, and nauseating special effects are *cut out* for various release prints. This often gives murder scenes a choppy, interrupted appearance and removes the very elements that a large segment of the audience has expressly come to see. While the gory scenes in the *Friday the 13th* movies are still pretty explicit, according to published reports they have usually been trimmed and toned down by the studio before release.

Splatter films with a supernatural basis are sometimes more imaginative than their mad-slasher counterparts. *The Evil* (1978) might have been a pretty good multiple-murder picture—horrible deaths occur in a creepy house which conceals an evil presence in the basement—were it not for the fact that said presence turns out to be a chubby, amusing, but hardly terrifying Victor Buono. *Wolfen* (1981) is an unusual and atmospheric tale of a race of mythical super-wolves who object to the tearing down of the dilapidated buildings they live in. It has marvelous trick effects (including special opticals that signify the wolfens' viewpoint) and a really horrific climax set on Wall Street. *The House Where Evil*

Albert Finney takes aim at a killer *Wolfen* in this gory supernatural thriller.

Dwells is about ghosts possessing the inhabitants of a house in Japan. It begins with an opening massacre that becomes an interminable slow-motion orgy of severed limbs and flying heads that is gross without being exciting. It gets *worse* after that. *Terror* concerns the murders of the actors making a witchcraft picture. Director Norman P. Warren exhibits an almost unhealthy relish when crushing and mutilating the assorted members of the cast, but when will directors realize that there's more to a successful knifing scene than intercutting shots of flashing cutlery and screaming mouths. The editing can't be done in a haphazard manner; it has to be *crafted* by someone who knows what he or she is doing.

Easily the best of the supernatural splatter films is *The Evil Dead* (1983). When five young people go up to an isolated cabin in the woods for a little vacation, they discover a "book of the dead" made of human flesh, as well as a tape recording of the demonic spells and chants inscribed therein. They play the tape recorder, the earth trembles, and *voilà!*—they are possessed by evil forces. To

An example of the striking visual quality of the energetic, entertaining supernatural "splatter" flick, *The Evil Dead*.

make matters worse, the only way a possessed individual can be stopped is to be totally dismembered. The hero of the film, Bruce Campbell (who gives a credible performance), is busy fighting for his life against his transformed, murderous friends for most of the running time; at one point even the trees of the forest come alive (the only sequence that really doesn't work). What keeps this perverse stew of mutilated limbs, gouged-out eyes, and dripping gore from being totally repellent is that the victims—the demon-possessed young people—look so *inhuman* at the moment of their deaths (indeed from the moment of possession) that the elaborate, visceral horror becomes almost comic-bookish; the distasteful proceedings can be watched with some distance, with an appreciative eye for the chilling and largely effective special makeups. The eye of the camera spares us nothing: corpses riddled with maggots, severed limbs, squirting blood, and tearing flesh. The gruesome makeup and mechanical and optical effects are mostly excellent.

Much of the credit must go to director/writer Sam Raimi, who has turned a low-budget gore opus into an exciting, grisly classic. Good camera work, fast-paced action scenes, and a lot of startlingly original touches lift this far above the usual exploitation level. *The Evil Dead* isn't art, but it is undeniably cinematic and a rare treat for those with the stomach for it.

Then we have general mad-slasher movies that don't fit into any particular category. *Silent Scream* (1980) features Yvonne De Carlo as the mother of a lobotomized woman (Barbara Steele) who comes down from the attic at night to murder the tenants in a boarding house. There are a couple of rousing stabbing sequences, but it's never explained just how someone who's been *lobotomized* can be so violent. *My Bloody Valentine* (1981), directed by George Mihalka, is a fairly decent shocker about a maniac, loose in a small mining town on Valentine's Day, who hacks up victims with a pickaxe and sends their torn-out hearts to the chief of police; only a perfunctory attitude during key scenes keeps it from being a top-drawer item. *The Comeback* (1978) involves Jack Jones with a nutty old crone who likes to dismember people with a scythe. A scythe-wielding harridan also shows up in *Curtains* (1980). *Butcher, Baker, Nightmare Maker* and Michael Loughlin's *Strange Behavior* (1981) are also notable, the former for its more unusual story line, and the latter for the surprisingly good notices it received.

Many films of the late seventies/early eighties period were inspired by Tobe Hooper's *Texas Chainsaw Massacre*. There was the *Mardi Gras Massacre*, the *Drive-In Massacre*, the *Hollywood Meatcleaver Massacre* (the promised meatcleaver never makes an appearance!), the *Slumber Party Massacre*, the *Zombie Island Massacre* (with Rita Jenrette), and a *Slaughter in San Francisco*. In other films of the period, people were stalked in forests (*Terror in the Forest, Don't Go in the Woods, The Final Terror*), on islands (*Humongous*), in deserts (*Death Valley*), on highways (*Road Games*), and burned to death by pyros (*Don't Go in the House*). Some were victims of *The Toolbox Murders*, the *Driller Killer*, or even man-eating *Pigs*. Others ran into *The Mutilator* and wound up in *Pieces*.

Meanwhile foreign filmmakers continued to pick up on American trends and make monstrosities of their own. Lucio Fulci has made a career out of aping George Romero's *Dead* films. His *Zombie* (1979) is a handsomely photographed imitation of *Night of the Living Dead* set on an isolated island where a voodoo curse has made the dead crave the flesh of the living. Fulci creates the usual disgusting havoc for the camera to wallow in: gouged-out pieces of flesh, spurting jets of blood, etc. One scene he did with obvious relish (not to mention an excruciatingly slow pace and solemnity) details what happens when a zombie pulls a woman's head towards a broken door and impales her eye on a jagged piece of wood.

The gruesome low-budget independent films mentioned in Chapter Seven are still being churned out, even grislier than before, in an effort to compete with the mainstream product. History does repeat itself: In both American and foreign productions, aging and "has-been" actresses *and* actors have been showing up when least expected in stalk-and-slash/splatter films. Hands down, the award for "most bizarre comeback" has to go to Carol Borland, who appeared in *Scalps* forty years after entering Horror Hall of Fame as a vampire in Tod Browning's *Mark of the Vampire* (1935), with Bela Lugosi.

While all this splashing and splattering has been going on, other kinds of shockers have been made in the seventies and eighties that don't rely on graphic bloodletting or the usual formulas to get their points across, though they can almost be counted on the fingers of one hand. *Murder by Phone* deals with a maniac who kills people over the phone, using electronic technology. (Sounds handy!) *Eraserhead* (1978) is the nightmarish, personal vision of director David Lynch, who later did *The Elephant Man* and *Dune*. It's still very popular on the "midnight movie" circuit, as is Frank Henenlotter's *Basketcase*, about the homicidal inhabitant of a hamper!

Magic (1978) is a flimsy concoction about a deranged ventriloquist (Anthony Hopkins) who, dominated by the personality of his malevolent dummy, commits the usual murders. *Looker* (1981) stars Albert Finney as a plastic surgeon whose beautiful clients are being systematically murdered after coming to him, with computer printouts listing their negligible flaws. Director/writer Michael Crichton keeps things consistently entertaining, and the story line makes creepy and fascinating use of modern-day technology, but the movie eventually crumbles under its contrivances and implausibilities.

Still of the Night (1983) is director/writer Robert Benton's (*Kramer vs. Kramer*) attempt to create the kind of smooth romantic thriller once done by Hitchcock. In it Roy Scheider plays a psychiatrist who finds himself falling for the lovely girlfriend (Meryl Streep) of a murdered client—only to wonder if she might be the one who killed him. *Still of the Night* is a suspenseful, eerie, and atmospheric thriller, well-crafted by Benton and well-acted by Scheider, Streep, and the supporting cast. Benton doesn't do as much with some scenes as he might have, but others, such as Scheider's scary encounter in Central Park, work beautifully. The denouement is rather perfunctory, though, almost springing out of nowhere and hinging on a rather far-fetched clue. Even the worst stalk-and-slash flick has a more exciting climax. Otherwise, *Still* is a nice exercise in style and tension.

Blood Simple (1985) is an overrated thriller about a bar-owner who hires a private detective to rub out his philandering wife and the bartender (John Getz) she's taken up with. Amidst much atmospheric tedium, the film does have two very striking sequences: when Getz buries his employer alive in the middle of an empty field after going through hell to get him there, and the final suspenseful battle between the detective and the wife, which is enlivened by some imaginative gore. The movie's characters are fairly colorful, but utterly one-dimensional and decidedly unsympathetic. It's basically a low-budget horror movie dressed up as a crime drama, and on that level, works fairly well. Director Joel Cohen shows some promise.

"Stalk-and-slash" and "splatter" movies have gone as far as they can go. Every type of death imaginable has been lovingly recreated on the screen. Nothing is left to our imagination any more: disembowelments, beheadings, amputations, entrail eating. Nothing is out of bounds. Most of today's horror filmmakers have an almost childish obsession with outdoing one another and coming up with the ultimate gross-out. Sadly, the clever editing and brilliant use of music that made *Psycho* so memorable is almost always absent.

Perhaps Hollywood can't—and shouldn't—go back to the simpler days of subtlety and restraint. (For one thing, it would be a shame to completely exclude the more vivid, graphic styles of today, which can be very effective.) In the long run, it is not how much blood is or is not spilled on-camera, nor how the bloodletting is presented, that matters. Hopefully more filmmakers (and their audiences) will come to realize that there is no substitute for a good story line, professional acting, and adroit direction and editing. Schlock may be good for a few laughs—but not much more than that.

Joan Crawford poses with her axe for this publicity shot for *Strait-Jacket*.

THE BEST AND THE WORST: TEN REPRESENTATIVE FILMS

The ten films in this chapter (a few of which were previously mentioned in passing) are candidates for the Horror Hall of Fame and Infamy. They are *not* a list of the "ten best," but were chosen rather because they are a good cross-section of the shocker at its best *and* worst. These pictures, with their assorted strengths and weaknesses, will help illustrate what the genre is all about.

In chronological order: *Strait-Jacket* (1964) is a quintessential American shocker of the sixties, while *Blood and Black Lace* (1965) is its stylish Italian counterpart. *Bird with the Crystal Plumage* (1970), another Italian film, put horror specialist Dario Argento on the map, while *Sisters* (1973) did the same for Brian De Palma. *Texas Chainsaw Massacre* (1977) is one of the most widely discussed horror films ever made, eliciting comment even from people who have never seen it. It and *Communion* (1977) are prime examples of what a talented director can do even with a very low budget. *Alien* (1979) is an example of what a shocker can look like when it's made on an *enormous* budget (while remaining true to its origins). *Maniac* (1981) is a "classic" women-in-danger film, the type that arouses the ire of feminists everywhere. *Nightmare* (1981), a gruesome stalk-and-slasher, contains scenes of violence that are startlingly horrendous and clinical. *Night School* (1981) is a quintessential eighties thriller that contains all of the obligatory elements of contemporary shockers.

Half of these films feature the antisocial acts of female maniacs, three of male mass murderers, one of both male *and* female killers, and one of an alien creature of indeterminate sex (probably female). Half of them are rather good pictures, at least two are only fair, and three are downright awful.

Strait-Jacket (1964). Produced and directed by William Castle; Screenplay by

Robert Bloch; Cameraman: Arthur Arling; Editor: Edwin Bryant; Music: Van
Alexander. Running time: 93 minutes. A Columbia Pictures release.
With: Joan Crawford (Lucy Harbin); Diane Baker (Carol Harbin); Leif Ericson
(Bill Cutler); Rochelle Hudson (Emily Cutler); George Kennedy (Leo Krause);
John Anthony Hayes (Michael Fields); Howard St. John (Raymond Fields);
Edith Atwater (Mrs. Fields).

Strait-Jacket is a quintessential American shocker of the sixties in both style and
(lack of) substance. Less sensual and colorful than European products of the
decade, it makes promises of violence (WARNING: "STRAIT-JACKET" VIVIDLY
DEPICTS AXE MURDERS" ran the ad copy) but doesn't quite fulfill them. It's as
callous and sensational as the *New York Post*, but it still gives you a thrill or two,
unencumbered by lofty aspirations to art. It's schlock stuff served up with relish
if not talent.

Strait-Jacket is of interest for at least three reasons. It was directed by William
Castle, one of his flamboyant follow-ups to *Homicidal*, and yet another attempt to
outdo Hitchcock. It was written by Robert Bloch, who tried unsuccessfully to
recreate some of the macabre humor that Stefano and Hitchcock put into *Psycho*;
it's a typical Bloch script in that it's gruesome, cold-blooded, and has a neat if
implausible twist at the end. It stars Joan Crawford, and so qualifies as one of the
"aging-actress" thrillers of the period. Crawford gives more than the picture
deserves. Though many found her performance overwrought, it perfectly fits
the disturbed, haunted character she is playing.

Lucy Harbin (Crawford) comes home from a trip one night and discovers her
husband in bed with another woman. Not one to go for the subtle approach, she
picks up an axe, whacks off both their heads (shown only in silhouette), and
proceeds to chop them up. (During this sequence the camera remains fixed on
Crawford.) Years later she is released from the mental institution and goes to live
on the farm of her brother Bill (Leif Ericson). Also on the farm are Bill's wife
and Lucy's daughter, Carol, whom the pair have raised since that fateful
evening. Carol is now an attractive young sculptor, played by Diane Baker.

But there are signs that Lucy Harbin is perhaps not yet ready to step out into
polite society. At her daughter's encouragement she dresses up in a wild, racy
manner like she did twenty years before. She makes a flagrant pass at her
daughter's boyfriend, Michael (John Anthony Hayes), and spills coffee all over
herself when she has dinner at his parent's house. To make matters worse, her
psychiatrist—who has come for a visit and is convinced that Lucy should go back
with him to the crazyhouse—is beheaded by an assailant. Then the obnoxious
handy man (George Kennedy) discovers the headless corpse in a freezer and gets
his head lopped off, too.

But when the axe-wielding maniac does the chop-chop routine on Michael's father, Lucy decides enough is enough and unmasks the perpetrator as . . . Carol! (The poor girl witnessed Mommy's massacre that night and has hated her ever since.) She knew that Michael's parents would never approve of her marriage to him (due to her mother's sordid background) and so figured she could dispose of them and make it look as if Mom had returned to her old ways. She was also behind various attempts to scare and torment Lucy.

Lucy accepts all this calmly and quietly, as if it were the most natural thing in the world, and plans to move back into the insane asylum to help her daughter recover. (Talk about the blind leading the blind!)

Luckily the film is so generally inept in most departments that it's impossible to take its lurid, hopeless, infinitely depressing story line at all seriously. Most of the picture operates on the level of travesty, a send-up of the genre, which is what Bloch may have had in mind—though probably not what William Castle did. Van Alexander's music is awful. It announces each scary or violent moment as if he were doing a parody of a horror film on the *Carol Burnett Show*.

There is one decent, suspenseful sequence when Castle really rises to the occasion, and that's the death of the handyman. Castle handles it all in nail-biting fashion, holding off the actual axe stroke until the very last second. The location of the scene is perfect: a meat storage room with lockers full of butchered beef vaguely seen through the misty glass. The frozen corpse of the psychiatrist, arms crossed as if the meatlocker were his coffin, is a chilling sight, and the murder itself—the lopping off of an obvious dummy head—is almost amusing. If Castle had handled the entire movie the same way he handled that one scene, *Strait-Jacket* might have amounted to something.

As it is, the film has a firm place in shocker history as a campy, corny harbinger of things to come.

Blood And Black Lace (1964). Original title: *Sei Donne per L'Assassino*. Directed by Mario Bava; Screenplay by Mario Bava, Marcello Fondato, Giuseppe Barilla; Director of Photography: Ubaldo Tersano; Music: Carlo Rustichelli.
With: Eva Bartok, Cameron Mitchell, Mary Arden, Arianna Gorini, Claude Dantes, Harriet White, Francesca Ungaro, Lea Kruger, Nadia Anty, Mara Carminoso, Heidi Stroh.

If one were to say that the Italian director Mario Bava had ever made a classic—albeit a minor one—it would have to be *Blood and Black Lace*, a multiple-murder mystery set in Rome. It is the definitive Italian murder mystery, the one that set the standard for most of those that followed.

Much of the action takes place at the Christian Fashion Salon in Rome, where

Eva Bartok collapses over the body of her dead lover Cameron Mitchell in *Blood and Black Lace*.

the body of a model, Isabella, is discovered tucked away in a closet by the proprietress, Christiana (Eva Bartok). Another model, Nicole (who had recently inherited Isabella's boyfriend), is then brutally murdered in the basement of the boyfriend's shop. Another model, Peggy, who has stolen Isabella's diary from Nicole, is at her home when the killer appears and demands to see the diary she's just thrown away. Scratch one Peggy.

Nicole's body has been discovered, Peggy is missing, the ladies at the fashion house are terrified, and the inspector assigned to the case is busy rounding up the various suspects, including Max Morlan (Cameron Mitchell), who apparently runs the business end of Christian Fashions.

Another model, Greta, who lives alone outside the city, is assured by Christiana that there is "no longer any danger" now that all the men associated with the salon are in custody. Surprise!—Greta is the next victim. Since a killing has taken place while all the male suspects were safely locked away, the inspector has no choice but to release them. Christiana is pleased to see Morlan again. No wonder—it seems she murdered Greta herself just to remove suspicion from the person she knows killed the other women: Morlan!

Isabella had been blackmailing Christiana and Morlan because of the suspicious circumstances surrounding the death of Christiana's late husband. Nicole and Peggy were killed because of what they might have seen in Isabella's diary, and Greta was killed to confuse the police. Morlan convinces Christiana that another murder must take place if they are to be cleared of all suspicion—the police think it's the work of a sex maniac—and though Christiana recoils at the idea, she agrees to carry out his plan. But after drowning yet another one of her models in the victim's own bathtub, she hears a frantic banging on the door and assumes it's the police. She tries to escape through an upper floor window, but falls when the drain pipe rips away from the wall.

Morlan, who had deliberately done the banging in order to bring about Christiana's demise (seems he knew about her escape exit and the weakened drain pipe, and wanted her to take the blame for *all* the murders), is shocked to find that Christiana survived the fall by landing on a shop awning. She shoots him, then collapses over his body after calling the police.

Blood and Black Lace is atmospheric, colorful, and nicely compact at 88 minutes. Besides being a quintessential Italian thriller, it is notable for its violent scenes (usually cut for television), which are more in the style of today's chillers. In the early sixties only Hammer horror films and gory American independents were conspicuously graphic, but the former involved vampires and monsters and were all quite comic-bookish, and the latter were too cheap and sleazy to take seriously. While *Blood and Black Lace* has a gaudy, neon prettiness, derived from its elegant and beautiful lighting, its murder-disfigurement scenes are pretty strong. Ubaldo Tersano's cinematography is often very striking, no doubt influenced by Bava, who used to be a photographer himself. His films are usually distinguished by a marvelous (if somewhat garish) use of color.

Carlos Clarens, in his excellent *An Illustrated History of the Horror Film*,[12] studied Bava's work and came to the following conclusion: "Recently, Bava has turned out a series of sadistic films, among them *Sei Donne per L'Assassino (Blood and Black Lace)* . . . [which] has minimal plot and consists of a string of brutal murders, each staged with relish and in the most redolent hues, attesting to the fact that Bava is simply trying to titillate a very specialized segment of his audience that requires neither rhyme nor reason." Considering how many gory shockers are made today, that "specialized" segment of the audience is either growing in numbers, or is not quite so specialized anymore.

Tony Musante and Suzy Kendall try to share a romantic moment in *Bird with the Crystal Plumage*, but Musante's mind is on the killer terrorizing the city.

Bird With the Crystal Plumage (1970). Written and directed by Dario Argento; Produced by Salvatore Argento; Director of Photography: Vittorio Storaro; Music: Ennio Morricone; Running time: 98 minutes. Released by UM Film Distribution, Inc.
With: Tony Musante (Sam Dalmas); Suzy Kendall (Julia); Eva Renzi (Monica); Enrico Maria Salerno (Morosini); Mario Adorf (Berto); Renato Romano (Dover); Umberto Rano (Ranieri).

The *Bird With the Crystal Plumage* is the film that first brought Italian terror director Dario Argento to American attention. The picture reveals a definite Hitchcock influence: unusual settings, oddball characters, hidden clues, and underlying meanings, all spiced with ironic situations. Argento is far from being a master of suspense, but in the acclaimed *Crystal Plumage* he has provided us with a decent, occasionally striking, often compelling exercise in the macabre.

Tony Musante plays an American journalist living with his girlfriend, Suzy Kendall, in Italy. Walking home to his apartment one night, he passes by a trendy art gallery and witnesses an attempted murder: A man in a raincoat and hat struggles with a pretty long-haired woman. She is stabbed, the assailant runs away, and Musante stays and tries to help the woman, only to be locked inside the outer foyer to helplessly await the arrival of the police and the victim's husband (who owns the gallery). Although the woman was not seriously injured, she is believed to be the latest in a line of females who have been brutally attacked by a killer terrorizing the city.

Musante, who is at first a suspect in the case, later decides to investigate on his own. Something about the whole case, about what he witnessed, bothers him, but he can't quite put his finger on it. Attempts are twice made on his life. Meanwhile, the series of murders continues: One woman is attacked in her bedroom and another cornered as she climbs the deserted staircase of an architecturally striking edifice.

Musante learns that the killer's first victim, a woman who worked in a gift and antique shop, was murdered not long after selling a modern painting that depicted a girl being stabbed to death in the snow. The killer makes a taunting call to the police, then another call to Musante, warning him that his girlfriend will become the next victim if he doesn't stop his investigation. A sound specialist informs the police that the calls were not made by the same person. He is, however, unable to identify the strange noise that can be heard in the background of each call.

An associate of Musante's borrows the tape and identifies the noise as the sound made by a rare species of bird that normally lives in Siberia. One of these birds, a rather large creature with white feathers that look almost like ice or glass (hence the "bird with the crystal plumage"), is on exhibit in a zoo located in the city. Musante, having interviewed the art gallery owner on one occasion, knows that the man's apartment is located directly across the street from the zoo, and that his phone is on a table near the window; the bird's noise could indeed have been overheard on that telephone.

Musante and the police arrive in the apartment to find the gallery owner and his wife engaged in a violent struggle. Convinced the husband is the killer, the police try to grab him, but during the tussle he falls out the window to his death. Before he breathes his last, he confesses his guilt to the police.

But there's a final twist: Musante finally realizes what was bothering him all along—it was not the man in the raincoat (actually the gallery owner) who was being the aggressor that night, but the man's wife, whom he had disarmed and stabbed in self-defense. She turns out to be the actual killer. Her husband had continually been covering up for her out of love, going so far as to confess to her crimes with his dying breath and to make one of the two phone calls attributed to the killer. In the climactic scene, Musante winds up in the gallery where the whole adventure started, pinned under a huge piece of sculpture that has been released from its mooring by the murderer. The woman takes out her knife and teases the trapped Musante with the blade. Just as she's about to deliver the death-blow, the police arrive to subdue her.

It turns out that the murderer was the victim of the brutal assault that inspired that morbid painting. Seeing the painting in the shop unleashed a dormant psychosis in her, but instead of identifying with the victim, which she had been, she identified with the assailant, thus initiating her psychotic killing spree of pretty young women. Musante and Kendall, in the meantime, board a plane for America—and after all they'd been through, who can blame them?

Plumage is not a perfect movie by any means, but it is a perfectly respectable offering, at least a cut above others of its ilk. The pace is reasonably fast and the movie is consistently suspenseful. The picture somewhat lacks the polished quality of U.S. productions, that special flair brought about by solid budgets and technological advantages, but the photography and editing are still quite good for the most part. The main flaw with the film is its insipid, jazzy musical score, which does absolutely nothing for it. A completely new musical background, composed by someone like Jerry Goldsmith, could turn *Plumage* into a whole new picture.

The murder scenes are the weakest sections of the movie, filmed in an "arty" style that fails to deliver the goods, as if Argento were trying different tricks without first seeing if they would work. He films a scream by starting with an extreme closeup of the tongue in the woman's mouth, then pulling back to show us her face. An interesting approach, but it doesn't increase the terror of the moment or make more vivid the woman's fear. In *Psycho*, Hitchcock cut from Janet Leigh's face to a closeup of her screaming mouth to pull the audience into the scene. Argento achieves the opposite effect. In fact the huge tongue filling up the screen looks silly. (Hitchcock didn't go so far as to stick his camera into Janet Leigh's mouth.) Another scene is simply a static hand-held shot of the killer lashing out at a cringing girl with a straight razor. Argento doesn't employ the tight, rapid cutting that these murder scenes cry out for.

This is not to say, however, that the movie doesn't have plenty of fine moments. The two scenes in the gallery—the struggle between the owner and his wife at the beginning and the finale with the wife and Musante—are both very clever and exciting. The scene when Musante pursues the hitman hired by the gallery owner to kill him ends on an amusing note. The assassin, wearing a yellow raincoat, ducks into a hotel. Musante follows him inside only to find himself in the midst of some sort of convention—and all the men are wearing similar yellow raincoats.

Pictures like *Plumage* are not meant to be examined too carefully. We might wonder why the killers in these films all have to wear black leather gloves, and have sinister, hidden rooms full of demented memorabilia. The psychology is *always* dubious. But perhaps that's irrelevant when one ponders the inescapable fact that *Crystal Plumage* is highly entertaining and well done for its type.

Sisters (1973). Directed by Brian De Palma; Screenplay by De Palma and Louisa Rose, based on De Palma's story; Produced by Edward R. Pressman; Music by Bernard Herrmann; Director of Photography: Gregory Sandor; Editor: Paul Hirsch; Distributed by American International Pictures. Running time: 92 minutes.
With: Margot Kidder (Danielle Breton); Jennifer Salt (Grace Collier); Charles Durning (Joseph Larch); Bill Finley (Emil Breton); Lisle Wilson (Philip Woode); Barnard Hughes (Mr. McLennen); Mary Davenport (Mrs. Collier); Dolph Sweet (Detective Kelly).

Although Brian De Palma had done other successful films before *Sisters*, this was the one that brought him to the attention of the critics and public alike, and which established him as a horror director of note. *Sisters* is an uneven film, one more of promise and missed potential than of any particular élan. The story, though an intriguing one, is a little shopworn, and some interesting aspects aren't as well developed as they could have been. Nevertheless, *Sisters* gets off to a rousing start, as De Palma was lucky enough to snare the talents of no less than Bernard Herrmann to score the picture. It is not one of the composer's best scores, of course, but is properly jangling and exciting in its own electronic way.

Sisters is about voyeurism if it's about anything, and De Palma constantly returns to this motif throughout the picture. The first scene takes place at a game show in which contestants must guess what a man in an awkward situation—his movements recorded by hidden camera—will do. Danielle, a pretty French model (Margot Kidder), enters a dressing room the man is in, allegedly unaware that it is already occupied. She is pretending to be blind. Will he turn away chivalrously, or watch her while she strips?

The man wins a night for two at a restaurant, the model, a set of steak knives. After having dinner together they take the ferry to Staten Island and spend the night at Danielle's apartment. The next morning Danielle mentions that she lives with her twin sister, Dominique. It is their birthday. When Danielle sends the man, Philip, out to get some medication, he impulsively decides to buy the women a cake. When he returns, she is still lying in bed. He puts the cake on a

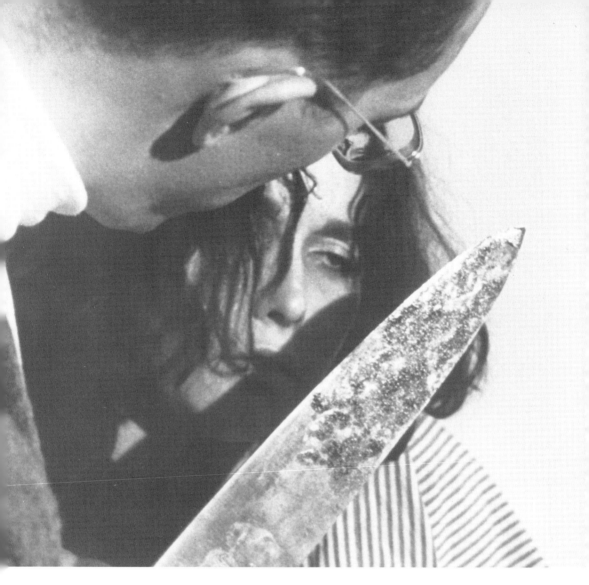

Bill Finley shows Margot Kidder the bloody knife with which she murdered an innocent man in *Sisters*.

plate, lights it, grabs one of the knives that Danielle won (much larger than necessary), and walks slowly toward the bed. Just as he positions the cake in front of the supine Danielle, so that she can blow out the candles, the woman suddenly grabs the knife and repeatedly plunges it into him.

  If the scene is shocking, it is probably due to three things: the unexpected change in tone, a gross shot of the knife stabbing straight into the victim's screaming mouth, and Herrmann's blaring, mind-blasting music. Otherwise, it does not have the kind of editing or energy that distinguishes the shower scene in *Psycho*. Most of the scene actually consists of the victim painfully dragging himself across the floor to the window where he scrawls *help* on the glass with his own blood.

From across the street the movie's heroine (Jennifer Salt), a reporter, sees the man dying in front of her eyes. The police are skeptical when she calls them, but do agree to meet her in the lobby across the street and search the model's apartment. Unbeknownst to them, Danielle's husband (Bill Finley) has arrived at the apartment, seen what happened, and hidden the body in the sofa-bed.

While Danielle's husband frantically cleans up traces of the murder, the police slowly make their way to the apartment. It is during this sequence that De Palma abruptly switches to a split screen. One side follows the cops and reporter, the other Danielle and her busy husband. Instead of increasing suspense, however, this device only serves to minimize it. For one thing, the audience is constantly aware of how close the police are.

The reporter insists that she saw another woman, a deranged type, in the room with the dying man, but pretty Danielle insists that she lives alone. Without a body or evidence of a crime, all the police can do is leave, so the reporter sets out on her own investigation with the help of a private detective (Charles Durning). Looking through a file Durning steals from Danielle's apartment for her, the reporter finds an article on famous twins written by a magazine journalist (Barnard Hughes).

At the journalist's office, the reporter is shown a short documentary on Siamese twins. This is one of the best sequences in the picture, and Herrmann's extremely ominous background music adds to it enormously. (Some feel the whole sequence is needlessly sensational.)

The reporter learns that Dominique and Danielle were recently separated after years of being joined at the hip. Dominique died on the operating table, or shortly thereafter. Danielle is apparently a schizophrenic who occasionally imagines herself to be her own sister, and who lashes out in hatred and confusion at anyone who gets in her way.

When the reporter goes to the clinic where the deranged woman had been staying, the doctor who runs the place (Danielle's husband) convinces the attendants that the reporter is a new arrival. Drugged and strapped to a bed in a room with Danielle, the reporter experiences a nightmare in which she takes the dead sister's place: the doctor makes love to Danielle while her sleeping sister is still attached; he performs the operation (with a meat cleaver, no less) while the crazed inmates, the private detective, and others look on. (This nightmare is another very imaginative sequence.) By deciding to clear up some loose ends in this bizarre, surrealistic manner, however, De Palma makes certain the audience is never quite sure what's fact and what's fantasy.

The doctor hypnotizes the reporter into believing that she did not see a body or a murder from her window. Not much later, he is dispatched with a scalpel in the belly by the awakened, once-again-maniacal Danielle, whom he had brought back to the clinic. Danielle is led away by the authorities. The reporter, confused and shaken, goes home to recuperate. When the police come calling, now convinced that her story was true, all she can do is repeat, "There was no body because there was no murder," over and over again.

Sisters has a lot of flaws. It has a somewhat slow pace, as well as too many ambiguities, loose ends, confusing parts, and cliches. In spite of these negative points, and its low-budget filming, *Sisters* still has its moments. It won't do anything to promote understanding of Siamese twins or schizophrenics, but it has more than enough thrills, imaginative moments, and interesting musical interludes to stand out among the competition.

The Texas Chainsaw Massacre (1974). Directed by Tobe Hooper; Produced by Hooper and Jay Parsley; Screenplay by Hooper and Kim Henkel. Released by Bryanston Pictures. Running time: 87 minutes.
With: Marilyn Burns (Sally); Allen Danziger (Jerry); Paul A. Partain (Franklin); William Vail (Kirk); Teri McMinn (Pam); Edwin Neal (Hitchhiker); Jerry Lorenz (Pickup Driver); and Gunnar Hansen.

It's become quite respectable to admit to enjoying *The Texas Chainsaw Massacre*, because the picture—despite its crudity and almost nonexistent budget—is a rather diverting, frequently exciting wallow in horror and perversity, courtesy of Tobe Hooper. *Chainsaw*'s parallel to *Psycho* is that both were inspired by the true-life deeds of Wisconsin mass murderer Ed Gein.

Chainsaw has been sensationalized and criticized—unfairly—because of its gruesome subject matter and that horrendous (if completely appropriate) title. The picture is not an exercise in restraint, true, but neither is it the super-excessive, vomit-inducing mess some proclaim it to be. Compared to *Singing in the Rain, Chainsaw* is enough to send many patrons screaming for the exits. Compared to most other horror films (especially those made afterward, and many made before), however, *Chainsaw* is fairly tame. There's plenty of gory violence in the story line, but most of it is left to the imagination. Whenever things threaten to get too bloody, the camera discreetly moves away or the scene changes. An axe comes down, but the audience doesn't see it embedded in anyone's head. The chainsaw prepares to slice through a person's flesh, but the camera doesn't show the victim. For the most part, the violence is left to the imagination.

The film concerns five luckless youths who come into contact with a family of homicidal morons. The most conspicuous of the lot is a chubby youth (Gunnar Hansen) who wears a leather mask. This overweight monster is fond of chasing after people with his chainsaw and dispatching them forthwith.

A family portrait of the deranged characters in *Texas Chainsaw Massacre*.

Sally Hardesty, her crippled brother Franklin, and their friends Pam, Kirk, and Jerry, have traveled to the country in their van to find out if the remains of grandfather Hardesty have been disturbed after the latest in a series of graverobbing incidents. After leaving the cemetery, they pick up a deranged hitchhiker, stop at a gas station that has no gas, and finally arrive at the now-uninhabited mansion that Sally and Franklin grew up in.

Pam and Kirk go off for a swim, then decide to ask at a nearby house for a can of extra gasoline. There they are set upon by the maniacal Hansen, who drags them into his workroom, hangs the girl up on a meathook, and proceeds to carve up her boyfriend with his favorite toy. Jerry goes looking for them and gets axed for his trouble. Once darkness falls, Sally and Franklin set off in search of the others, only to run smack dab into Hansen, who slaughters Franklin and runs maniacally after Sally with murder on his mind, chainsaw *buzz-buzzing*.

Sally manages to run back to the gas station, only to discover that the middle-aged proprietor is related to her pursuer. To make matters worse, the deranged hitchhiker is in the family, too. Sally is invited to stay for dinner, rather forcibly, and is literally tied to her chair at the supper table. She manages to escape, but not before being again pursued by the chainsaw killer in the movie's most thrilling episode.

Hooper creates an eerie atmosphere right from the start. The picture begins in total darkness, which is punctuated now and then by the bright light of a flashbulb; someone is apparently taking pictures of a bunch of rotting corpses. Graverobbers (actually the hitchhiker) have been at work; they have even draped the body of one poor soul over a monument. The young people arrive at the gravesite and Sally is relieved to discover that her grandfather's remains have not been disturbed.

The sequence between the visit to the graveyard and the arrival at the old abandoned home has many interesting aspects to it, but it goes on too long and is not filmed with much élan. The doomed youngsters notice a horrible odor in the air, only to learn that the road passes right by the slaughterhouse, an ominous foreshadowing indeed. When they pick up the half-crazed hitchhiker, who is on his way home from the same slaughterhouse, he shows them grisly pictures of dead cattle, more (somewhat obvious) foreshadowing. It is also during this drive that the film's bloodiest sequence occurs, when the hitchhiker, possessed of a sudden, inexplicable mania, slices the palm of his own hand with his knife. (Hooper lets the blood dry too quickly, however; such a wound would have bled for quite some time.) Thus offending the group's sensibilities, he is thrown out of the van, but not before slashing Franklin's arm with the quick stroke of a razor.

Once Hansen makes his appearance in the second half of the film (a rousing moment to be sure), the action is non-stop. The man in the mask jumps out unexpectedly—no sudden creeping or idle spying for him—

A young lady tries to hide from the maniac who has murdered most of her companions in *Texas Chainsaw Massacre*.

bangs his victims on the head (the early victims, at least), and then drags them posthaste into his little "workshop," slamming the sliding metal door to his chamber of horrors like a petulant child protecting his goodies. While most of what happens then is left to the imagination, the butchershop imagery is striking and horrifying. The final section of the film (and perhaps the most distateful), deals with the torment of the only survivor of the thoroughly disordered family. This scene is also a little too long, and Hooper doesn't help any by trying to convey Sally Hardesty's encroaching madness by overdoing the closeups of her bulging eyeballs. She sits tied up at the dinner table while the three loony captors eat their supper and taunt her. They mimic her cries and struggling motions and tell her what they're going to do to her. The film loses all control when the brothers' old granddad is brought down the stairs. The grandfather looks just like a corpse, and audiences always seem perplexed when he starts to stir after Sally's cut finger is shoved into his mouth and he begins to slowly—then greedily—suck the blood out of it. Can this wizened old creature actually be alive? Apparently he is. (The body of the old man's wife, whom we can assume is genuinely deceased, is also kept upstairs in a horribly disheveled chamber.)

The scene where granddad is enlisted to kill Sally is black humor at its funniest and most grotesque. The younger men in the family push Sally to her knees and put a bucket underneath her head. Still sitting above her, granddad is given a hammer with which he is to knock her into the next world. It seems he, too, used to work at the slaughterhouse, and when cattle were killed the old-fashioned way, he was one of the best headbashers in the business. Unfortunately—or fortunately, if you look at it from Sally's point of view—granddad hasn't quite got the stuff anymore, and the heavy hammer keeps falling out of his hand. He does get in one good blow, but it's not enough to kill her. Instead, Sally is able to break away and crash through the window and get outside. To the audience's surprise, it is daylight now; she's been tied up for hours.

The last few minutes of *Chainsaw* are wonderful, a rapidly edited and thrilling chase, as Sally is pursued by Hansen and the hitchhiker onto the highway. The driver of the Mack truck that comes along and runs over the hitchhiker is a big, hefty fellow. When Hansen starts after him with the chainsaw the picture takes on an almost comical overtone, without ever losing its edge-of-the-seat quality. The pace doesn't let up until Sally finally makes her getaway. The truck driver runs out of the picture, while Sally narrowly escapes the stinging kiss of Hansen's saw by jumping into the back of a passing pickup.

That the film ends with the chainsaw killer still standing loose on the highway, waving his chainsaw, is either a nice way of scaring the audience (who will he be coming after *next?*) or merely indicative of a budget that has run its meager course.

Chainsaw received odd reactions, ranging from fascinated, if overly analytical, adoration, to unmitigated outrage. Those offended by its violence have either not really seen the picture or have seen no other horror movies of recent vintage; there is actually less blood spilled *on camera* than in *The French Connection* or *Bonnie and Clyde* (much less than the latter). Critics could harp at the tacky quality of the lensing, the many washed-out shots, the dull filming of the long drive in the van, a general low-budget sleaziness that's one step above home movies. Yet, the film has enough clever, imaginative touches (to say nothing of its sheer energy), to lift it far above the bottom of the barrel. As a parody of hideous family life—its antagonists representing virtually the antithesis of what is considered sane, decent, and moral—it has no peer. The macabre sets, particularly the cluttered, reeking insides of the house, with its bones and grease and tatters, the steel door in the "workroom" that shuts with such grim and grisly finality, are quite evocative of horror. The soundtrack, with its odd bells and noises, is disturbing and appropriate. And the acting, while sometimes over-done, is wild enough to fit the surroundings. The high-pitched chattering of the masked killer, in such contrast to his fat but formidable appearance, is a nifty touch. Devotees of sick humor will surely number *Chainsaw* among their favorite films, yet it is also a favorite of fans of the purely horrific.

Communion (1977). Directed by Alfred Sole; Screenplay by Sole and Rosemary Ritvo; Music by Stephen Lawrence; Produced by Richard K. Rosenberg; Running time: 96 minutes.
With: Paula Sheppard (Alice); Brooke Shields (Karen); Tom Signorelli (Detective Brenner); Louisa Horton (Psychiatrist); Mildred Clinton (Mrs. Tredoni); Linda Miller (Mother); Jane Lowry (Aunt); Niles McMaster (Father); Rudolph Willrich (Priest); Alphonse De Noble (Landlord); Gary Allen (Uncle); Michael Hardstack (Detective); Lillian Roth (Pathologist).

Communion takes place in 1961 in New Jersey, where it was filmed. Alice (Paula Sheppard) is a rather plain young girl who is resentful of all the attention being paid to her pretty little sister, Karen (Brooke Shields), who is just about to make her first communion. Before the girl can do so, she is attacked and placed unconscious in a chest, which is then set on fire. The priest and nuns run to investigate the horrible odor, and find the poor youngster's smouldering body. Alice is suspected of her sister's murder, as well as of the other slayings and attacks that follow.

Thus begins Alfred Sole's *Communion* (retitled *Alice, Sweet Alice* by its distributor), which starts out as a kind of *Bad Seed* spin off, but soon turns into a riveting, well-made tale of murder and madness set against the background of the Holy Roman Church. "I wasn't making any statements about the Church," Sole told *Cinefantastique*. "It was only that milieu that I wanted to use."

Nevertheless, *Communion* has been regarded by some as an attack on the oppressive values of the Church that are passed down from one generation to the next. The film ends with the apprehension of the actual killer after she has plunged a butcher knife into the neck of the priest presiding over communion. That the bloodied knife is picked up and hidden away by a younger, equally disturbed member of the parish cannot, some feel, be without significance. The hypocrisy and helplessness of Alice's family's religious contacts are constantly contrasted with scenes of grisly and furious violence. In a sense this picture is the antithesis of all those Church-versus-evil pictures in that the evil *is* the Church.

Ulterior motives and meanings aside, what counts in *Communion* is the handsome way in which it has been made. It doesn't have that obvious cheapjack look that so often ruins the atmosphere of other productions made on a low budget ($400,000). Though full of the usual loose ends and absurd situations, this oddball little movie is done with such enthusiasm and skill that it amounts to a superior and thoroughly entertaining shocker, complete with a twist wind-up and generous dollops of suspense. The screenplay, by Sole and Rosemary Ritvo, incorporates Gothic elements that are by now too much an integral part of the thriller genre to be taken as clichés.

Just about everything in *Communion* works, but even when things go wrong it works in the picture's favor. Sole's direction is at times a bit overwrought (intentionally?) and the picture and characters more grotesque than they need to be. Sole overuses closeups, but at times even this affectation, such as during a confrontation between Alice's mother and Alice's aunt after the first murder, increases the sheer weirdness of the movie. Sole has peopled the film with actors who are either already bizarre to look at (young Alice; the grossly obese landlord, Alphonse De Noble), or makes the more attractive cast members look strange with exaggerated makeup and hairstyles. Linda Miller, who plays Alice's mother, is a pretty actress who walks through most of the film with a hairdo that sticks out from either side of her face and suggests she's no more normal than the rest of the cast.

Among the stand-out sequences in the picture is a scene wherein Alice's father is trapped by the killer, gets his face bashed in, a cross thrust down his throat, and is eventually thrown out of a building. The knife attack on the aunt when she comes down the stairs is particularly notable—a series of well-edited shots of a flashing weapon stabbing into the woman's legs and feet while she tries to dodge the blade on the landing above. Sole knows how to build tension and suspense and how to effectively depict violence without being overly dependent on gore.

The actors are quite good, too, especially Paula Sheppard as Alice. Jane Lowry as the aunt tends to overact (which is saying something in this picture) but Mildred Clinton hits the right note as the disturbed Mrs. Tredoni. Brooke Shields has little to do in the film, but her appearance in it (after rising to fame via Calvin Klein ads and movies like *Pretty Baby*) elicited a re-release of the picture in 1981 under the title *Holy Terror*. Portly Alphonse De Noble is nothing if not original, and the late Lillian Roth makes a very brief appearance as a pathologist. Stephen Lawrence's music recalls Bernard Herrmann, but is undeniably effective.

Communion remains one of the very best and most unsual horror films of the past quarter-century.

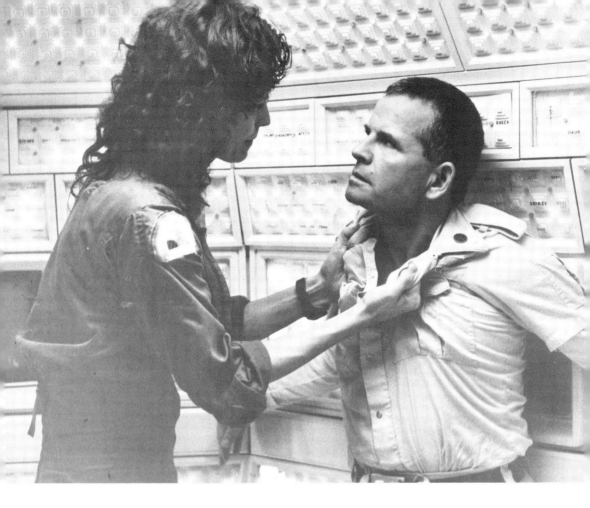

Ripley (Sigourney Weaver) confronts the robotic Ash (Ian Holm) in a tense moment from *Alien*.

Alien (1979). Directed by Ridley Scott; Screenplay by Dan O' Bannon, from a story by O' Bannon and Ronald Shusett; Produced by Gordon Carroll, David Giler, and Walter Hill; Executive Producer: Ronald Shusett; Music by Jerry Goldsmith; Edited by Terry Rawlins; Director of Photography: Derek Vanlint; Production Designer: Michael Seymour; Art Directors: Les Dilley and Roger Christian; Alien Design: H.R. Giger; Alien Head Effects created by Carlo Rambaldi. A 20th Century Fox release. Running time: 124 minutes (Panavision; Dolby Stereo).
With: Tom Skerritt (Dallas); Sigourney Weaver (Ripley); Veronica Cartwright (Lambert); Harry Dean Stanton (Brett); John Hurt (Kane); Ian Holm (Ash); Yaphet Kotto (Parker).

Alien is an intense, frightening monster movie that substitutes a horrible, shape-changing space creature for the usual homicidal maniac picking off his or her victims one by one. That's really all there is to it, though the movie's slender premise is backed by stunning art direction, clever special effects, and one of the most unusual monsters—a blend of the biological and the mechanical—that has ever munched its way across the screen.

A spaceship with a crew of seven sets down on a planet to answer what they think is a distress signal, but which turns out instead to be a warning. In what should have been short order, but which takes too long under Ridley Scott's ponderous direction (particularly in the early scenes), the ship picks up an alien life-form that jumps out of a sort of pod or egg casing and attaches itself to the face of a crewman (John Hurt). When they try to cut the small, tentacled thing off of the comatose fellow, it drips acid that eats through several levels of the ship. Finally the thing shrivels up and drops off, and the crewman returns to normal. He joins his co-workers as they eat their evening meal.

Then comes a sequence that may one day be as infamous and imitated as *Psycho*'s shower murder. It seems the tentacled thing deposited another life-form inside the man's body, which at a well-timed moment *bursts out of* the man's stomach and, needless to say, kills him. This alien life form then slithers off to hide in the nooks and crannies of the ship. Occasionally it makes a horrific reappearance in order to turn the other six crew members, aside from the one survivor (Sigourney Weaver), into hamburger.

The picture is good, scary fun, but it's not very logical. The monster grows in size at an unprecedented rate, and goes through more metamorphoses than the audience can keep track of. The ship's medical officer turns out to be a robot. He explains that, unbeknownst to the crew, picking up and bringing the alien to earth was their primary mission. How the owners of the ship knew of the alien's existence, or what they would possibly want with it, is never explained.

Still, along the way there are plenty of gruesome shocks and chills, including a creepy scene of a crewmember being attacked by the thing in a conduit through which he has been crawling. The basic premise of stalk-and-slash has been embellished with fascinating, sinister elements, handsome production values, good ensemble performances, and a nice musical score from the talented Jerry Goldsmith.

The picture was never as controversial as *Psycho* was in its day, but it did elicit a similar kind of outrage from some critics. Wrote David Denby in *New York* magazine: "Occasionally one sees a film that uses the emotional resources of movies with such utter cynicism that one feels sickened by the medium itself. *Alien*, the new monster movie, is so 'effective' it has practically turned me off movies altogether . . . yes, it's only a monster movie, but the way it manipulates the audience is rather sinister."

The "chest-burster" scene, which is clinical and graphic, offended certain critics and some of the audience, though most people thought it was just a macabre, clever shock that took everyone by surprise. Many people thought *Alien* was simply a rip-off of fifties and sixties science-fiction terror films like *It, The Terror From Beyond Space*, and Mario Bava's *Planet of the Vampires*. There are undeniable similarities, though neither of those films, nor *any* of the genre from those earlier decades, were quite as well produced and striking as *Alien*.

Other critics felt the story of *Alien* was simply too trivial to bother spending so much money and employing so much talent on (designer H.R. Giger's contributions are particularly noteworthy). Perhaps Scott and his crew are to be commended, however, for making such a handsome and compelling thriller instead of just another schlocky low-budget monster movie.

Maniac (1981). Directed by William Lustig; Screenplay by C.A. Rosenberg and Joe Spinell; Story by Joe Spinell; Director of Photography: Robert Lindsay; Edited by Lorenzo Marinelli; Music by Jay Chattaway; Produced by Andrew Garroni and William Lustig. Released by the Analysis Film Corporation. Running time: 91 minutes.
With: Joe Spinell (Frank Zito); Caroline Munro (Anna D'Antoni); Gail Lawrence (Rita); Kelly Piper (Nurse); Rita Montone (Hooker); Tom Savini (Disco Boy); Hyla Marrow (Disco Girl); Tracie Evans (Street Hooker); Sharon Mitchell (Second Nurse); Carol Henry (Deadbeat).

Maniac (at least the third film to have that title) contains one scene that is modeled after the Son of Sam killings, but the villain of the film much prefers stabbing and scalping to shooting. He is Frank Zito (Joe Spinell), who was beaten and abused by his mother as a child, and therefore, so the movie suggests, hates all women, most of whom are apparently off-limits as far as he is concerned. The picture begins with him killing two lovers on a beach. He garrots the boyfriend, with such force that the man is lifted bodily off the ground, then zeroes in on the girl for more nasty "pleasure."

Frank lives alone in a cluttered room full of department-store dummies, which he presumably steals when no one is looking. The film is little more than a series of gruesome incidents. First he takes a hooker to a hotel room and strangles her (in a rather energetic scene which, for once, does not make strangling someone seem easy), then cuts off her scalp in full view of the camera. Next he pursues a nurse through the subway and corners her in the bathroom, stabbing her in the belly. The scalps of the women he kills are lovingly draped over the heads of the mannequins at home.

Next our "hero" meets the beautiful and charming Anna D'Antoni (Caroline Munro, poor thing), who is a top fashion model. For unaccountable reasons

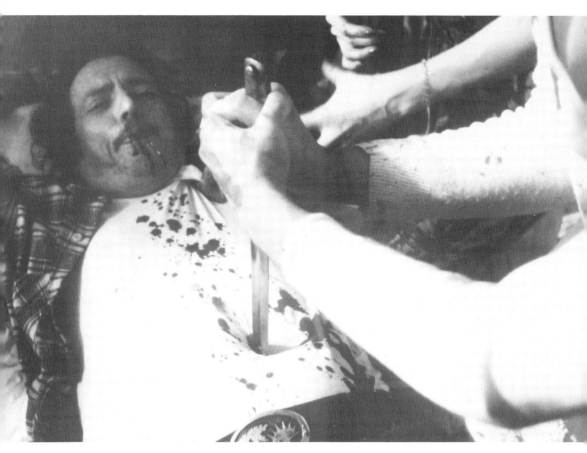

His victims get revenge on Frank in *Maniac*, or is that just the audience telling Spinell what they think of his acting?

Anna is attracted to Frank and agrees to go out with him. While he waits for her to finish up at a photo session, he hears strains of "Goin' to the Showdown." The song is a reasonably nifty rock number that musically suggests the mix of sex and violence that *Maniac* is aiming for (more violence than sex, it would seem). Although Frank Zito is portrayed as a loser who must kill women because they frustrate him, he has no trouble picking up a sexy beauty like Munro. So much for logic.

Frank slips out one night and sneaks up on a pair of lovers who are parked on the side of the road, necking. He blows the man's head off (a truly vomitous exhibition), then gets to work on the fellow's girlfriend. The man, by the way, is played by Tom Savini, the makeup artist who did all the gory effects for this film (and many others), including his own exploding head.

Anna is not quick to realize that something is wrong with her new friend, Frank, even though he has killed one of her model-friends. She finally gets the message when he takes her to the cemetery to visit his mother. He hallucinates that a hand has come out of the grave to grab him, and naturally goes berserk. Intrepid Anna grabs a shovel and whacks him on the head with it, the only woman to fight back and therefore the only one to escape.

The film's most memorable moment—in terms of the macabre—is the final sequence, in which the dummies in Zito's apartment come to life, gather around his bed, and literally rip his head off—his many victims getting their revenge. This, too, has been a hallucination, because the police find Zito still in one piece the following morning.

The movie is low-budget, but professional. Exceedingly grim stuff, it is that grimness, that unrelenting intensity, that makes *Maniac* so disturbing, more so than the gore. It is that quality that makes the film notable; on virtually every other level it is strictly grade-C.

Maniac's cleverest aspect was its saturation ad campaign, including the movie's poster and slogan. The ads pictured the bottom half of a man—holding a knife in one hand, a head dripping blood in the other—and the line, *I warned you not to go out tonight*. The illustration had to be doctored considerably to get into the more restrictive papers.

Reviews of *Maniac* were merciless. Vincent Canby summed it up in *The New York Times*:[13] "Good sense, if not heaven, should protect anyone who thinks he likes horror films from wasting a price of admission on *Maniac*." He went on to say: "Watching [Joe Spinell] act like a psychopathic killer with a mommy complex is like watching someone else throw up."

Spinell's performance, while more than adequate for the purposes, often draws laughs when he suddenly starts sobbing alone in his room after slicing someone up. Spinell wrote the story and collaborated on the screenplay, so he's more than a little accountable for the final product. William Lustig's direction is generally tedious, but Robert Lindsay's cinematography is often better than the picture deserves. Critics who have complained that the film is squarely in the mold of other sexist, kill-the-pretty-women pictures are undoubtedly on target.

Lorenzo Carcaterra, interviewing Spinell in the *New York Sunday News*,[14] had the last word. Spinell told him about his dream of starting a production company in Astoria. "I hope Joe's dream comes true," wrote Carcaterra. "If nothing else, it will keep him from making low-budget horror movies. Just the thought of one less *Maniac* loose in this city is more than enough to make me sleep better at night."

Nightmare (1981). Written and directed by Romano Scavolini; Director of Photography: Gianni Fiore; Music by Jack Eric Williams; Edited by Robert T. Megginson; Produced by John L. Watkins; Executive Producer: David Jones;

Production Supervisor: Simon Nuchtern; Sound Mixing: Mike Russell; Special
Effects Makeup: Les Larraine and Ed French. Running time: 97 minutes.
Released by 21st Century Distributing Corporation.
With: Baird Stafford (George Taturn); Sharon Smith (Susan Temper); C.J.
Cooke (C.J. Temper); Mik Cribbon (Bob Rosen); Kathleen Ferguson (Barbara);
Danny Ronan (Kathy, the babysitter); John L. Watkins (Man with cigar).

This notorious horror movie (one of several to use the title *Nightmare*),
denounced by one critic as "the most depraved movie ever made," is a gloomy,

The mad killer of *Nightmare* (Baird Stafford) holds his knife and waits for another victim.

Nightmare's killer puts his latest slashing victim in the trunk of his car.

depressing, darkly atmospheric piece of junk that somehow manages to transcend its hack origins in the last twenty minutes. *Nightmare* is a behind-the-scenes look at the lives of several characters who are caught up in an ever-widening spiral of horror. It chronicles the events brought about by an awful tragedy, the type sensational newspapers exploit for all its seaminess.

The movie's villain, busy stalking his wife and son while murdering a string of mostly female victims, began his sick career as a child, killing his parents while they were too busy making love to defend themselves. The villain's son is a tow-headed curmudgeon who delights in telling tall tales and frightening his mother and her boyfriend, as well as his siblings. The implication is that his mind is already becoming as unsound as his father's.

Make no mistake: *Nightmare* is not some deep drama, nor a profound, tragic look at life's bitter misfits. For most of its length it's simply another trashy, rather badly made stalk-and-slash film, and a tedious one at that. Then, in the final minutes, we see the picture's *raison d'etre*: the flashback scene showing the double murders committed by the father when he was a boy. They are staged in excruciatingly explicit detail, lovingly and bloodily presented with exact precision, like a carefully crafted advertisement.

The little boy is slapped by his abusive mother. He watches from outside the bedroom door as she and her husband engage in some sado-masochistic pleasure. She ties the man to the bed, sits on him, and slaps him repeatedly. Looking as if his morals have been somehow offended by his mother's violence, the boy gets an axe, re-enters the bedroom, and whacks her in the neck with it. Blood gushes out. Another blow—and her head flies across the room. His father screams, tries to explain; it was just a game. Standing on the bed the boy repeatedly hacks at his mother's body, then raises the axe for the final time and slams it down into his father's forehead.

The sequence is undeniably repulsive, but strangely haunting, almost beautiful in its ugliness. The boy's white shirt is soaked with red gore, the white walls are streaked with it in exotic patterns. The boy (cast to perfection) sits there with an intense, lost, angry, *numb* look on his face. *Nightmare*, as bad as it is, is perhaps the only terror flick within memory that actually makes a shocking, gruesome incident look tragic and momentous instead of merely horrifying. The boy seems both aware and unaware of the enormity of what he has done.

For illustrating, without flinching, the story behind a morbid incident of the kind one skims through in the daily papers, then represses, *Nightmare* is a very grim movie indeed. The picture ends with another tragedy—the father dead, the boy unhinged, his mother screaming out in shock when she learns the identity of the now-dead killer. The only thing that spoils its completely despairing, without-hope effect, is the way the director figuratively winks at the audience with a closeup of the boy smiling in the back seat of the police car (like the end of *The Omen*, only more exaggerated).

The uncredited, angelic-looking blond boy in his nicely pressed clothes who plays the murderer as a child must be noted, as well as the poignant music at the end of the slaughter scene, which was composed by Jack Eric Williams.

Night School (1981). Directed by Ken Hughes; written by Ruth Avergon; Director of Photography: Mark Irwin; Editor: Robert Reitano; Music by Brad Fiedel; Produced by Larry Babb and Avergon; A Lorimar release through Paramount Pictures. Running time: 88 minutes.
With: Leonard Mann (Judd Austin); Rachel Ward (Eleanor); Drew Snyder (Vincent Millett); Joseph R. Sicari (Taj); Nicholas Cairis (Gus); Karen Mac-Donald (Carol); Annette Miller (Helene Griffin); Bill McCann (Gary); Margo Skinner (Stevie Cabot); Elizabeth Barnitz (Kim Morrison).

A helpless victim is about to be slashed to death by the maniac in *Night School*.

Night School came near the end of the initial "stalk-and-slash" cycle, and it seems the director had learned his lessons well; it contains all the *de rigueur* elements of the psycho-shocker and then some. *Night School*'s most effective aspect is its grim atmosphere, helped enormously by location shooting in Boston. The subject matter is more distasteful than usual, dealing with a series of decapitations committed by an assailant who wears motorcycle gear and a large black helmet that obscures the killer's face.

Police are stymied by grotesque murders of young women in Boston; their heads have been removed and then submerged in water. The second victim was a student at a girl's college, and provides the investigating detective with his first substantial lead. It seems she was a student in a young professor's anthropology class, and possibly one of the man's many girlfriends. The teacher is quite the tom cat, apparently, a personality trait that does not sit well with his assistant and live-in lover, Rachel Ward.

Ms. Ward is followed home from a restaurant across from the college by a dim-witted fellow employed there as a busboy. In yet another scene that pays homage to *Psycho*, someone sneaks up on Ward while she showers. (The camera movements also ape Hitchcock's film to some extent.) The furtive figure, however, turns out to be her amorous roommate, who gets in the shower with her and smears her with reddish goo—some sort of ritual lovemaking he learned from the natives, one assumes.

A third victim, killed at her job at the oceanarium, is attacked in the locker room after getting out of her wet suit. Meanwhile, the professor and his lovely assistant have problems of their own. While grabbing a bite to eat at the restaurant, Ward scolds him for playfully flirting with the waitress, a friendly, middle-aged bleached blonde. Then she hits him with the news that she is pregnant. That night, while closing up, the waitress is attacked. She's feisty and puts up a good fight, but eventually succumbs.

The detective goes to see the professor and notices some books on headhunting in the man's office. He learns from Ward that headhunters believed that submerging the heads of their enemies in water would free the heads of evil spirits. That night the headmistress of the college where the professor teaches is cornered and killed by the maniac. Her young lover finds the older woman's head floating in the toilet bowl in the bathroom, and is then herself dispatched by the killer, who sneaks up silently behind her.

The killer turns out to be Rachel Ward. Pathologically jealous, she has been killing any woman her lover had a real or imagined attraction to. She somehow convinces him to get into her clothes and take her place on a motorcycle (in an offscreen scene), where he attracts the attention of the police and is killed in the ensuing speedchase. The detective suspects that the case is not closed, but as he can't prove anything, Ms. Ward goes off a free woman.

If nothing else, *Night School* is unique in that the killer—instead of dying under a hail of bullets, getting decapitated à la Betsy Palmer in *Friday the 13th*, or dying in some grisly, revenge-motivated manner—walks out of the picture (after attending her late boyfriend's funeral, of course) with nary a care in the world.

This is not to say that *Night School* is any kind of women's lib picture. Although written by a woman (assuming the screenwriter's name is not a pseudonym), *Night School* contains all the usual ingredients of the stalk-the-pretty-girls-and-kill-them genre. The beautiful victims squeal, wail, cry, and shiver helplessly as the killer approaches and slashes them bloodily with a few preliminary strokes. And the killer herself is hardly a well-balanced, liberated individual, but is, rather, so tied to her man that she must slaughter anyone who even remotely threatens their relationship. She delivers a few lines about women fighting for what is rightfully theirs, but she's not talking about equal pay for equal work.

The screenplay also adds a gratuitous lesbian scene, probably for the same reason male porno mags feature pics of women together to titillate their readers. The lesbian character (the headmistress) is hardly a positive one. After a young woman complains to her about being used and dumped by the promiscuous professor, the headmistress announces her intention to fire him for fooling around with the lives of her students—then promptly hits on the girl herself, the old gay-as-molester stereotype.

Horror fans will find that *Night School* has a lot of interesting aspects to it, however. Its strong sadistic overtones are enough to satisfy anyone in need of violent emotional catharsis, and some of the murder scenes are clever, the first one in particular: The killer approaches the victim as she rests in a playground, sitting on one of those circular platforms that spin around. The killer reaches out a hand and starts the wheel turning. She waits until it is spinning faster and faster, then raises her blade to the victim's neck level, and applies savage force as the woman rushes past helplessly in a dizzying swoosh of motion.

A great deal of sickening suspense is also generated in a scene following the death of the waitress. The audience suspects that her head has been placed in a big pot of stew she was fussing over before facing the killer. The next morning the owner puts the pot on a stove, heats it, and serves two heaping bowlfuls to two hungry customers. "You should use a hairnet," one of them complains, pulling a mouthful of hair from his teeth. Disturbed, the owner goes back to the kitchen and begins to pour the stew from one pot to another. We expect the head to drop into view any second. It isn't there. The owner goes about his business, opening refrigerator doors and cupboards, the audience expecting the head to drop into view at any second. It finally turns up in the sink, at first hidden by grease and suds, but then revealed in all its grisly glory.

Although Ken Hughes' direction lacks style and vigor, he seems to know what he's doing for the most part; the film does have a professional look few other low-budget stalk-and-slash movies ever achieve. The performances are reasonably good. Rachel Ward was most striking opposite Steve Martin in the comedy spoof, *Dead Men Don't Wear Plaid* (she also starred in the TV miniseries, *The Thornbirds*). Here she is not photographed flatteringly, and her performance is only adequate. The theme music is nice and eerie, but isn't much used during the picture itself. Murder scenes are backed by the electronic "slash" music used so often in this kind of film.

Director Hughes has had a checkered career. He did a fine job with the excellent, literate *Trials of Oscar Wilde*, starring Peter Finch as the notorious Irish writer, then sank to rock-bottom years later, directing a half-senile Mae West in the abysmal *Sextette* (her last—and least—film venture). *Night School* is somewhere in between.

NOTES

1 There has always been confusion over the exact year of release for many films, with reference sources citing conflicting dates for films, often released at different times (and/or with different titles) in different countries. The release dates given throughout this book are generally based on the year the film opened and was reviewed in New York.
2 London: Faber & Faber, 1978.
3 Boston: Little, Brown and Co., 1983.
4 Hitchcock. François Truffaut. New York: Simon and Schuster, 1967.
5 A.S. Barnes, 1965.
6 Massachusetts: Harvard University Press, 1982.
7 *Psycho*, Richard J. Anobile, ed. New York: Darion House/Avon, 1974.
8 New York: G.P. Putnam's Sons, 1976.
9 "Where B Means Brutal," by Barney Cohen. Oct. 1984.
10 11 Feb., 1984
11 *Daily News,* Sunday, 25 Jan., 1981.
12 New York: Capricorn Books, 1968.
13 31 Jan., 1981.
14 25 Jan, 1981.

INDEX

1491